A devoted reader and passionate writer, Samuel Peckham had always dreamt of sharing the stories he created and has now achieved that with his debut novella, *Apocalypsis*. At twenty-five years old, he seeks a long and successful career in literature with so much to offer. Dark plots, mysterious characters and shocking twists, usually including some philosophical views and theories, is where Samuel feels most natural when he holds a pen. He describes his work as "romantic punk-noir". He also loves movies, music, football and tattoos.

Dedicated to my three favourite authors for influencing me the most: George Orwell, Chuck Palahniuk and Stephen King.

To fred

Hope you enjoy the book!

Samuel Peckham

APOCALYPSIS

AUSTIN MACAULEY PUBLISHERS™

LONDON • CAMBRIDGE • NEW YORK • SHARJAH

A CIP catalogue record for this title is available from the British Library.

ISBN 9781788485142 (Paperback)
ISBN 9781788485159 (Hardback)
ISBN 9781788485166 (E-Book)

www.austinmacauley.com

First Published (2018)
Austin Macauley Publishers Ltd™
25 Canada Square
Canary Wharf
London
E14 5LQ

*We can all agree that our numbers are too high, whilst the
wealthy jest, the rest of us sigh.
Those that make love are those that lose breath, those that
make life are those that meet death.
The trees were pulled down, and the land was drowned.
Elephants and whales bled, and the tears of many were shed.
There are plenty of us to spare, but not enough animals or
plants to share.
Our cancer may have been ceased, but we remain as Earth's
disease.
We read old books to gain sold knowledge, with new discovery
continuously foraged.
Those who do not believe in God now pray, for the war was
imminent and waged today.*

How It Happened
The Year Is 2057

The population of the human race is 12 billion.

Since 2055, it has been illegal to perform sexual intercourse. This is to prevent reproduction, which is viewed as the world's number one dilemma on the agenda. The punishment for this crime is execution.

Due to deforestation, most of the planet's forests and natural landmarks have disappeared, resulting in the extinction of numerous species. Due to the reduced amount of oxygen in the atmosphere and the copious amount of pollution created daily by our existence, there has been a major increase in health issues.

Antarctica has vastly diminished in the last forty years because of global warming.

War, poverty and famine are more severe issues than ever before in history.

Food shortage, due to increasingly high demands of growth, production and distribution, has caused worldwide starvation, even leading some individuals to resort to cannibalism.

Cannabis is legal worldwide but at a high price.

Aristocracy has been disbanded. No kings or queens, no lords or ladies, and no celebrities.

You are either rich or you are poor. There are no in-between classes.

The richest person in the world is the woman who cured cancer in 2043.

Teachers and surgeons are the highest paid members of all societies. Only certain people in particular areas are given priority for schooling and welfare. The rest of us must teach ourselves from old books and learn from our elders.

Art is no longer worthy or relevant. New literature, music, films and paintings are no longer affordable to anyone but the rich.

Robots control most work flow although some people are still expected to contribute, but the majority of people are unemployed and have to fend for themselves. This has caused an increase in crime worldwide.

Harvesting on the moon began in 2049. A mission to Jupiter in 2051 had given us hope.

Scientists are on the verge of discovering evidence of paranormal life and alien life.

The rest of us are searching for God.

The struggle of modern life has created arguments and disagreements between continents.

There is conflict in America, Europe and Asia; one might say there is tension in the black air.

We are a threat to one another. Everyone is claiming to be the superpower.

There are an equal amount of capitalists, communists, socialists and fascists all over.

The rest of us seek utopians.

But there is no time for dreams.

The world leaders meet and discuss the current situation on Earth, mankind's future and the prospect of making a ruthless decision in order for the human race to have a chance of survival and for the world to regain a smooth rotation.

We do not know who attacked first. We do not know who attacked last. We, us, the survivors, do not know much other than that we are alive, although that isn't such a good thing.

The doomsday clock stopped ticking as the time had arrived.

The red alert lights came on and the alarms were signalled.

The buttons were pushed and the missiles were sent.

The world waited…

Part I: The Bomb

Chapter 1

They were sat together on the tattered sofa, the only sofa they owned, squeezed tightly against each other whilst watching a repeat of an old television show that had originally been aired before any of them had been born, back when television shows used to be made frequently and when most people could afford to watch them. They were like most families in their area: they owned only three channels which played nothing but shows from over twenty years ago, whilst the rich were busy experimenting with their million pound toys and hologram walls.

All four of them snuggled up like herded sheep in the middle of the afternoon with the curtains drawn and with blankets wrapped round them, even though it was summer, because the house was always cold.

"We've seen this episode so many times," moaned the girl, who was eight years old.

"It's cool!" replied the son, three years older than her, as he turned with an angry expression.

She answered him back, he called her a name, she returned one, he hit her on the leg, she cried, the mum scolded him, he answered her back, and all the while the dad was fixated on the television in confusion and anticipation. The other three hadn't noticed the show had disappeared and had been replaced by a black screen with complete silence.

Suddenly, a yellow symbol appeared at the centre of the screen. The dad knew what that symbol meant: it was the warning sign for a nuclear attack. The warning sign the world had been expecting to see for a long time.

"Citizens of Great Britain," a calm but serious male voice spoke from the television.

"Be quiet!" shouted the dad, and then all eight eyes were glaring at the screen.

"This is a message brought to you by the Government. This is not a hoax, this is a warning. A nuclear attack has been declared. We are at war. All cities must be evacuated now. Do what you can to get to safety…"

The dad stopped listening. He was trying to think.

"What does this mean?" asked the mum, gripping him by the arm.

The dad ignored her and used the remote to switch over to the next channel and then the next and back to the first again. All three were broadcasting the same symbol and the same message being read by the same voice.

"Answer me!" cried the mum. The two children had stopped fighting and were now looking to their parents for clarification of what had happened to the television and why the adults looked so worried.

"It's happening," the dad said in a husky whisper to himself.

"What do we do?" asked the mum frantically.

"Mum, what's the matter?" questioned the girl.

"Is there another war, Dad?" came the boy's voice, almost excitedly.

The dad got to his feet and pulled open the curtains to stare out into the sky.

If we survive or not, this will be the last time we'll see the sky as blue as that, he thought. Due to the pollution of today the sky was always a strange blue anyway, more of a blackened blue with dirty clouds, but it was going to be the most beautiful they would ever see it again.

The message on the television had finished and then repeated itself in a cycle. An air raid siren from the town began ringing with a rising drone that lasted ten seconds before lowering and going round in a loop.

"Pack your things," ordered the dad with his back to them, peering out to the sky. "All you need is your clothes and food. Take nothing flammable! We're leaving this house in two minutes."

He turned to find the three of them standing frozen, staring at him.

"Go!" he yelled. The two kids ran to their bedrooms to fetch what they could.

"Where are we going?" asked the mum, closing in on him with teary eyes.

"We're going to be fine. I'm going to make sure of that," he promised and then kissed her gently.

The mum headed to the kitchen and followed his orders as she packed tinned food and bottled water.

The dad grabbed a first aid kit, dust masks, his mobile phone, some batteries, and a watch, before piling everyone into the car (they were only one of two families that lived down their road that owned a car, and it was only a forty-year-old Volvo Estate), as he prayed inside his head that the engine would not die on them.

"Are your seatbelts on? This is going to be a fast drive," said the dad. The kids nodded.

"What is your plan?" tested the mum.

The dad turned on the engine and pulled out of the driveway.

"When will we be coming home?" whined the girl, almost on the verge of tears.

"Never, stupid! It's going to get blown up!" cackled the boy.

"Don't scare your sister!" growled the mum through her teeth.

"Where are we going, Dad?"

The dad breathed out to catch his breath and thoughts. *Every dad in the world has the same responsibility as me right now*, he supposed.

"We're going to your great-grandfather's house in the country."

"Why?" queried the girl.

"Because it's a lot safer there," he replied, looking to the mum who didn't express agreement.

As long as we get there in time we might have a chance, he thought.

The drive would be about forty minutes, thirty if he was quick and could get out the city before most people tried to evacuate.

His grandfather's house had an old underground shelter that had been used by his ancestors in World War Two over a century ago.

"A new world is dawning," he said quietly without meaning to speak aloud.

"What?" asked the mum.

"Nothing."

Chapter 2

He watered his flowers in his garden. The siren had been ringing for an hour but it did not affect his daily routine. The old man had decided that his life was almost over anyway and that he'd had a better life than a lot of people, having been born in the previous century, and he was thankful for that. His wife had died over fourteen years ago, he had no one else in his life, nothing to live for. He did not mind leaving now.

I'm too old to run, he thought, as he sprinkled the glistening water out of the can and over the heads of a dozen lilies. They had been his wife's favourite flower.

His house was in the middle of Paris and he knew he didn't have a chance.

This world isn't like it used to be, he confirmed, shaking his head, almost chuckling to himself over the thought.

But then he froze and straightened up, as straight as he could be with a bent back from years of hard work, and by raising one hand as a shelter above his eyebrows he glanced upwards, squinting from the sunshine which made the lilies glisten as they swayed in the gentle breeze.

The first of the jets he had been expecting came flying over, so low he could almost see his reflection in the black metallic underbody of the plane, so fast it caused what little white hair he had left on his head to switch direction, and so loud its screeching growl deafened him shortly, blocking out the siren that was ringing, and when it had passed it left behind an excitement under his flesh and a reassuring numbness he hadn't felt for a very long time.

I'll be with you soon, my love, he whispered in his mind, as he smiled up at the sky before returning to water his flowers.

Chapter 3

Their television screens on the plane had activated the alert. The captain had told them to remain calm. The return flight to New York still had another half-hour to go.

"Even if there is an explosion, it can't reach us up here, can it?" asked the woman, sat next to the man who anxiously peered out of his window.

"I don't think so," he replied, not removing his line of vision from outside.

He had just been on holiday for the last week, relaxing in Spain by himself. He could afford it, everyone on this plane was rich, or on any plane today for that matter. But he knew better than anyone that in this situation money did not matter, it could not save him or anyone: everyone was in the same boat together and the boat was sinking quickly.

"We're above the sea anyway," he replied. "We're in one of the safest places you can be."

"I've heard before that a nuclear explosion can be felt miles away. If there are several of them, won't the explosions or heatwaves eventually reach us?" she asked. It had probably been her hundredth question since the alert had come on.

He stared down at the deep, dark, deathly waves rolling over each other below him, and he imagined the plane plummeting towards it and having to let go of everything and accept his fate.

"I don't know about that," he replied, shaking his head.

"And what if it does happen and we are able to stay in the air; we'll have to land eventually. Where will we go?"

"I don't know," he said, losing his patience and wishing he had chosen another seat for what could possibly be his last few minutes of comfort.

A minute or two passed without either of them speaking and suddenly the glow he had been expecting and looking out for appeared in the far distance like a large lightbulb being dropped on the planet. It was as if a comet had crashed to Earth.

This is history in the making, he thought, *although there probably won't be anyone alive to write about it.*

"We've been hit," he whispered in disbelief, unable to retract his eyes from what he was seeing as he watched the overgrown mushroom cloud sprout.

"What?" asked the woman.

"America has been hit."

For some reason, maybe an act out of pure horror, he grabbed the woman's hand and held it tight. Although he could not stand her, if he was to die, he did not want to die alone.

Chapter 4

The mother shouted at her son when he returned home, ordering him to get inside. The fury inside of her wanted to scream at him with her boiling red face and saliva spraying, maybe casting a light backhand round his ear, but the motherly instinct of love and the sensation of relief that he was nearly in her arms and was safe, at least for now, gave her the urge to wrap herself around his tiny, innocent body and plant wet kisses all over his face.

The siren had been ringing in the small Indian village for an hour but the little boy had been playing with his friends in the middle of a field, unaware his poor mother had been frantically searching the whole road for him, calling his name, and putting her on the edge of tears even though she was a woman that very rarely showed a sensitive side.

When the siren had begun the boy and his friends had been by themselves, out of sight, without anyone to tell them what to do and what the siren was for, so they had stood still listening to it, unaware that all the other children had gone home or had been dragged indoors someplace.

The mother screamed again, this time at the top of her lungs, demanding he use his legs and run to her as fast as he possibly could, as he dawdled along the dusty path swinging a stick in his hand which he had been using as a pretend cricket bat on the field. He had once seen some of the elderly men in the village playing and had been told by one of them that cricket was what they used to call a sport, but only rich people could now afford to play and watch games.

The boy began to quicken his pace with the dust blowing around his feet, the siren now having caused a piercing white noise in his ears, and the sound of his mother yelling at him from a distance, knowing he was probably about to receive a stinging red cheek as the result of his mother's hard, grainy hands.

But all of a sudden he stood still, he ignored his mother, even the siren was now background noise. The dust continued to blow around him like a miniature tornado, but now it grew stronger and blew into his eyes as he painfully attempted to look up to the sky.

There was a whistling sound getting louder and louder, closer and closer. He figured, after a few seconds, that the sound was coming from the object that was falling from the black clouds, as if God had sent him a present.

The object was falling directly towards him. It was going to land on his village, it was almost aiming for him as if he were the target; the largest balloon he had ever seen.

The whistle had now become the loudest, most sickening sound he had ever heard, and would ever hear.

His mother's scream was faintly recognisable among the siren and the whistling which had turned into more of a thunderous screech.

It's a present from the Devil, the boy thought.

The boy did not flinch, he just stood in fascination and curiosity.

The last thing he saw was his shadow; his only imprint that would remain on the planet.

Chapter 5

"I don't think we're going to war. I don't think we'll get involved," said the first guy, sat opposite his friend in the café.

"Of course we'll get involved, we're Britain," replied his friend, the second guy, whilst sipping at his coffee, his elbows on the table, and leaning into the first guy's eyes where he found burning flames of fear that were trying to be watered down with confidence.

The first guy noticed the siren had been ringing for almost an hour as he checked his wristwatch. The television had made its announcement and had warned everyone to prepare for impact, but for people like them there was nowhere to go, there was nothing they could do.

"The television said…" the second guy was saying until his friend interrupted him.

"Fuck what the television said! They're just trying to scare us so we stay in line. It'll be between America, Russia and China at the end of the day, and to be honest as long as we're all right I don't really care what happens to the world anymore, this was inevitable and is probably for the best."

"You seriously believe that?" asked the second guy, keeping his hands warm by caressing his coffee.

The first guy did not respond immediately, he hesitated in thought as he peered over his friend's shoulder to examine the rest of the innocent people inside the café who had nowhere to run and were holding up here, cowering, crying and embracing one another.

They were in the middle of a prime target: London.

"Yeah, we'll be fine," he finally responded, but in his voice there was uncertainty.

He picked up his coffee with unsteady hands as the second guy watched him, almost sensing the vibration of his friend's heartbeat rapidly speeding up.

"My coffee's cold…" began the first guy with a grimace as he swallowed, but he was distracted by something in the corner of his eye.

The cup tilted on the edge of his finger and thumb as the liquid poured out onto the table. He gazed out of the window and into the distance with a gaping mouth and stretched eyes that did not blink.

It was like nothing he had ever seen, like nothing any of these people had ever seen.

"What?" asked his friend in a terrified tone as he turned over his shoulder to peer out the window.

Everyone saw it. Women screamed, children cried, men cursed.

Across the city, less than two miles away, a blinding glow of orange light expanded and rose in the bright summer afternoon, but it was not the sun, followed by a deafening thunder which drowned out any confidence and allowed the fear to burn.

It's just like the movies they used to make, was the last thought the first guy had.

Chapter 6

In the poorest area of Los Angeles, where people had long ago hurried to their places of concealment with the air raid siren having now been ringing for over an hour, a man was all by himself, running through a road with no knowledge of direction, having abandoned his car a mile back after he had crashed due to people flocking past him and distracting his attention.

He had been on a business trip and had been returning home, far from here, knowing, in a few hours, he would be arriving at his luxurious mansion, as he gazed out of his car window measuring the hideous image of the houses he was passing, if you could call them houses, until the siren had begun, followed by a swarm of desperate and frantic people storming the streets to get to safety, where he eventually veered off the road and met a tree.

Now he found himself stranded, all alone, petrified with not what was going to happen to this city, or his country, or the world, or his so-called family and friends, or the disgusting poor people he despised and usually jested about with his work colleagues, but petrified with what was going to happen to him.

At the last house on the road, which was more of a wooden shack, he noticed a closing steel door of what appeared to be a basement which led to some sort of shelter underneath the ugly building.

"Hey! Wait!" he cried, hurrying towards it with his suit and tie blowing about, and the suitcase in his hand swinging behind him.

The ajar door came to a halt and the hand did not move. He bent over to peer into the darkness below and met the eyes of a frail old man with a beard and one glazed iris.

"Please help me! Let me in! I have nowhere to go!" begged the rich man, perspiring and gasping for air.

"Do you have anything to offer?" asked the old man who was clearly poor like everyone else around here. He didn't know a single man that owned a suit.

"What? I need to come in! I'm going to die!" the rich man cried, almost angry that such a peasant could have control over him and his possible fate.

"Can you provide food, water or warmth?"

"Well…no, but…look…" he paused, opening his suitcase and exposing the dollar bills that lay inside. "I have money! You can have it!" he barked, desperately pushing it towards the old man's face, almost trying to force his way inside the basement.

"Us poor people have been preparing for this for years whilst you rich have forgotten of our existence and been busy playing with all the toys the earth could give you. You took everything and left us with nothing. You're responsible for this. Maybe you should think about that before your time is up, what you shouldn't be thinking about is trying to bribe the people you never cared for before. What makes you think we want money?" he laughed hysterically, joined by the laughter of several others inside the basement below which reached the rich man's ears.

"You can have it! It's all yours!" the rich man begged.

"We don't want it! Don't you see?" growled the poor old man. "There won't be money in the new world my friend, it's no good to us, it's no good to anyone, not even you!"

The door was slammed shut in the rich man's face and he heard several bolts slide into place. He cursed at them and kicked the door but then realised he was pointlessly wasting his time and energy. He was still stranded, he was still alone, the siren was still ringing, and the money in the suitcase was now blowing away in the wind, and for the first time in his life losing wealth did not faze him.

Then there was an explosion.

Chapter 7

He thought the ringing sound had been part of his dream. It wasn't until he heard the cry of his children's voices enter the room, begging him to wake up and pulling at his duvet, that he realised the siren was, in fact, real.

The young, single-parent man observed his children's scared faces before climbing out of bed and heading to the window.

He could hear the television's announcement that was playing from the other room and how it warned that his city, Hong Kong, was a target of a nuclear attack.

His two children, both young daughters, held a hand of his either side of him as he stared out into the city.

In the distance, there was a burning glimmer, it reminded him of a giant Chinese lantern, although he knew it wasn't one because it wasn't heading into the sky, it had come down from the sky and onto the land.

The flames appeared in his glassy teared eyes and he knew this was the end. He was no longer sleeping, he was wide awake, but for now, as he cowered with his two children, the thought that this would be the only nightmare any of them would ever have again and that they would share it together somewhat comforted him.

Birds fly.
Rats scurry.
Cockroaches crawl.
Humans stop and stare.

The World as We Know It
The Year Is 2061

The population is now predicted to be less than 2.4 billion; the lowest since the 1940s, which is around one hundred and twenty years ago, but it continues to decline. By the end of the Nuclear Holocaust, or the Apocalypse, or World War Three, or whatever you want to call it, the human population had been reduced by eighty percent.

Only two continents remain on the planet which are deemed habitable, the two continents that were least affected: Africa and Antarctica, although the radiation in the air would have reached them by now.

It was the collapse of civilisation with widespread destruction and radioactive fallout.

Modern technology and scientific advancements are at a standstill, there is a breakdown in society meaning communication between nations is limited, the economy has collapsed, cities have been destroyed, and the environment has been damaged resulting in nothing growing.

For two years, the surviving humans lived in underground shelters and basements, fending for themselves. Survivors continued to die due to health issues caused by exposure to radiation and the nuclear winter that had followed the war which had caused the average temperature on Earth to fall by six degrees Celsius.

In 2059, the remaining political figures ordered soldiers in military uniforms, with weapons and old vehicles, to search over the lands to rescue the survivors, or what some would describe as capture. Those found were given a number to represent them so the population could be recorded, although it was believed that many survivors were supposed to be living by their own accord, almost hiding, believing they'd have a better chance by themselves and not wanting to hand over their freedom, therefore choosing not to participate in the reconstruction and reproduction of the new world.

The rescued/captured survivors were taken to safety areas which were least affected by the war; mostly blocks of buildings in a surrounded area used to accommodate the survivors of society and to keep them within a sealed glass dome.

That's how the majority of the human race has been living for the last two years.

There is talk among them that one theory for the future is that the governments, or what is standing to be the governments, will, after a certain length of time, eventually escort all of the survivors to one of the two remaining continents that are habitable, or will spread them evenly across the two (although Antarctica is probably not an option for more than one reason), for societies to be reintroduced and for mankind to continue living.

But no superior figure has mentioned anything as such to the survivors. They have been left in the dark.

It's a new age.

Part II: The Vault

Day 741

Chapter 1

This is just the way life is now. That's what people are always saying.

I used to think it was crazy how anyone could be so lonely in such an overcrowded world. Now the world is smaller and I find myself living among too many.

Here in The Vault, that's what we call this place, there are sixteen of us living together. We are all men, all aged over eighteen, the eldest of us being a seventy-two-year old. Men, women and children are all kept separated. For what reasons? We are unsure, we don't receive any information.

Let me tell you a little bit about The Vault. We are located on the top floor of our building; an old construction of flats with ugly, grey paint flaking from the outside walls, the smeared windows are all caged on the outside to ensure there are no escapes, and The Door is locked twenty-four hours a day, only being opened when the guards enter to bring us food or very rarely to deliver mail that may have been sent by another survivor from another vault, or to resolve a problem that may have occurred within our group, or to remove a dead body.

We were much more overcrowded here before. Since being here, in two years, we have had two murders, seven suicides, nine medical related deaths, and one escape. There have also been three occasions when the guards have entered unexpectedly, grabbed someone and taken them away for us to never see again, the exact reason why we all suspect there is a spy within the group.

We receive only two meals a day: one at midday and one in the evening, and both of them are very measly, but at least we are being taken care of to some extent.

You receive one pack of cigarettes and a box of matches per week if you are a smoker, one bar of soap at the beginning of every third month, a dry towel at the beginning of every week, and a quarter filled flask of tea every day along with both meals. One shave a week if you wish to shave, one haircut every two months if you wish to have one, and only two pairs of clothes: at the end of each week you hand over to the guards the clothes you have been wearing for the last seven days and you receive the clean pair, then the following week it's the same process and you receive the first pair again which would have been washed.

Our only water supply is drinking from the taps in the toilet room.

The building that we are situated in used to be a block of flats which has had the walls from one end to the other completely knocked out to form one large living area running the entire length of the floor in order for us to all live here together, and there are twelve floors in the building all together, some may have more people living together than others, and there are another seven buildings just like ours scattered nearby, almost in a circle. We know this because we remember seeing how the place looked from the outside when we had been discovered by the military in 2059 (two years after the war) and had been brought here, but most of us know this anyway because we get the opportunity to see the outside now and then when we are chosen for labour, but I'll get to that in a moment.

It's possible that there are other vaults located around the country and that all of the survivors of Britain are to be designated to them, it sounds plausible and makes sense. Some of us have even had the terrifying thought that maybe the entire population of Britain (apart from the inevitable few that are still living somewhere by themselves and have not been discovered, or may have chosen not to be discovered to keep whatever freedom they believe they still have) could be living within these eight buildings, within the walls of these ninety-six floors. I am number 649 which means I was the six hundred and forty-ninth survivor of Britain to have been found and brought here, at least that's what we think our numbers mean, everything is a guess, because as I already said, we don't receive any information.

It's possible that there are only around one-and-a-half thousand people living within the eight buildings, within the ninety-six vaults, and that is our community. We rarely ever see anyone outside of our own floor though (outside of The Vault).

None of us have ever been informed as to how bad the war really was. We know it was bad, worse than bad, but we don't know how many people are predicted to have perished and what remains of the planet.

The area was not affected by the nuclear blasts and with the buildings still standing *they* used it to start forming a new society. Who are *they*? The area is surrounded by a glass dome which was sealed by the Government, not that we're sure who the government are anymore, and we believe it's been put there for one of two reasons: to prevent us from escaping beyond it and/or to provide clean air inside the dome to avoid any of us being affected by radiation, although we all know that *that* one is probably too late.

But it isn't too late to escape.

Everything that we talk of now is just theories, the authorities don't tell you anything.

There is freedom here in the sense that the guards do not disturb us unless for any of the reasons I have already listed, we are supplied entertainment such as old books, playing cards and a chessboard, and we are served our meals and kept safe from the dangers on the outside. Of course, all of that isn't good enough though, we want to step outside and see the world, we want to breathe and live.

There is only one form of labour, which is gardening. They are trying to plant and grow new greenery, plants and trees around our buildings within the dome. You can volunteer to participate by asking the guards to put your name down on the waiting list. There are some that have never volunteered and therefore have not stepped outside since arriving here two years ago. It's not even labour if it's volunteering, and to be honest being able to go outside and take part in something, other than sitting around all day talking and going mad, is a luxury. The only reason people call it labour is because it can be very cold outside.

More theories among conversations in The Vault over the last two years have suggested that the Government are using us as an experiment, testing us maybe for bodily reactions to radioactivity or the deprivation of natural air or the effects of confinement. I must confess I am the theorist of one of these. I believe that we were not rescued but in fact captured and we do not have our freedom because they are confining us and oppressing us, maybe in fear of there being further issues in the world among the survivors. I'm not too sure but if you live like this long enough you can't help but point the finger at someone, become overly creative and want your freedom.

Some of us even believe that there are cameras hidden inside our living space—maybe one inside a book in the playroom, maybe one in the corner of the main room, even one in the showers, possibly one watching us when we sleep, or another one behind the mirror in the toilet room?

The mail is one of the most favourite talked-about theories. Some of us also believe that if anyone receives a letter it could be a trap to see if any of us are planning something, or maybe if the letters are genuine then it's possible that the guards proof read them beforehand. When I arrived here I had asked them to check the names on the survivors list for me, just in case anyone I had cared about was living in another vault, but there was no one, and for that reason I have never received a letter. Everyone I had known is dead.

The mistake we made, I think to myself as I stare out of the window, was that there were too many of us to be able to work so we had to create something to take our place. With technology having become so advanced and with humans being so intelligent we created a robot which was an even smarter, faster, better functioning piece of equipment than the robots we had before, such as; computers and self-checkouts and machines and anything electrical, forcing us to become the slaves. Yes, we may not have had to work, but we were still the slaves because we were taking orders from the rich and the robots, we had to grow our own food and fend for ourselves. And when the robots had been programmed and taught to create an even better robot than itself, this forced us to become third-class citizens, the animals of the world, the bottom of the fucking food chain. We handed over our brains and the robots engineered and rewired them for their use. We killed our own intelligence and evolution.

I have to ask this one question: Is man intelligent? Seriously. Try and answer that question.

Our freedom was blown up with everything else.

"Elliott…" comes a faint, distant voice as I continue to stare out of the dirty window to my right, through the barred fencing surrounding it outside, struggling to see into the distance and beyond the dome, but it is not possible from where we live.

"Elliot…!" the voice speaks again, this time louder, startling me and drawing my attention away from outside and back to the room; my freedom being abandoned out there somewhere, outside of The Vault, outside of the dome.

"What?" I reply innocently as if I have been listening, my eyes meeting those of a handsome, balding, forty-something-year-old black man called Kris.

"It's your turn," he says with a smooth voice, joined by a smirk and gawking eyes that are almost asking me where I had drifted off to for the last thirty seconds. He knows, and so do all of the others sitting round the small circular table, but nobody asks, nobody ever asks each other.

I glance at the cards I hold, without having much care for the game of poker, and sigh, "I'm out," I say, before laying them down on the table and pushing my chair out as the other four examine my cards.

We are sat in the playroom which is located through an open doorway from the main room. It's a small, square room with a wooden floor, a wall to the left separates this room from the bedroom, and behind me at the back of the room are three bookshelves and another small window which looks out towards another one of the buildings. We have noticed that in that building, on the floor that is eyelevel with ours, there are women living there.

I stand from my seat and walk past the window that is to my right, the one I had been staring out of, and head towards the doorway into the main room, but I am halted by an outstretched hand that has gripped the sleeve of my shirt.

We all wear the same clothes here which are supplied for us: a white shirt (long or short-sleeved, depending on what you chose when you first came here), navy blue jeans and black shoes, also a black, buttoned jacket which is rarely seen being worn by anyone seeing as the heating here is turned up so high all of the time (there must be a functioning generator in each building) to prevent us from dying from the blistering conditions of the outside world, so they're usually left draped over your bed, unless you're going outside for garden duty.

"Are you alright?" whispers George who is sat next to Kris, peering up at me, leaning back in his chair.

"I'm just tired," I reply, lying. I have no interest in playing cards, I have very little interest in anything anymore.

George gets to his feet and the other three at the table grunt as he deserts their game to join me as I head into the main room.

"What's wrong?" asks George as we stand by the windows.

George is the person I am closest to here and confide in the most. He is always making sure I am okay. He is a little shorter than me, his hair is greying, although he is only in his late thirties, probably due to modern life, and he has dark stubble and bright blue eyes.

"Nothing's wrong," I say, lying again as I avoid eye contact with him, regarding my surroundings.

The main room is the largest area of living space we have, being the majority of three flats joined together. It has been designed almost like an old changing room you would have expected to find in a sports centre many years ago. There are benches running round the whole length of the room with a couple more placed back-to-back at the centre. This is where the sixteen of us spend most of our time, although you do occasionally need to lie down on your bed because sitting upright all day causes serious back pains, and we also take it in turns as to who uses the table and five chairs in the playroom each day.

"You've been dreaming again, haven't you?" asks George.

"Hmm…?" I respond quietly, retracting my attention from everything else and returning it to George who is standing quite close to me.

"You can't keep thinking about the world and questioning everything. You have to think of yourself."

"I can't help it!" I snap, then lowering my voice. "No advancements or evolution in four years. What is there left for us to accomplish? Underwater civilisations? Colonising other planets?" I snort sarcastically. "No. When that button was pushed and the first missile was sent, it was one small push for man but one giant pull for mankind. 'The Bomb' has ended our civilisation. We've fallen back by centuries."

Everyone here in The Vault refers to the nuclear war, to the missiles and to the button being pushed as 'The Bomb'.

"Elliott, you need to stop living in the past mate," says George.

"The past is the only place to live. There is no future."

"Is that really what's bothering you?" he asks in a tone as if he hasn't been listening. I pause for a moment before responding.

"No, it's just…this place," I say, shaking my head.

"I know how you feel, we all feel the same. Nobody wants to live like this. But you have to remember," he is now whispering, turning over his shoulder a couple of times to make sure no one is listening to our private conversation, "it's only a few more days until we get out of here. The hole is nearly dug and we'll be gone, leaving this place behind. Okay?"

I think of the hole which George is referring to. The hole we have been slowly digging for the last four months which only the two of us know about. For the last four months we have been volunteering to participate in garden duty and every now and then one of us, on occasion both of us, have left The Vault for a few hours and have used the gardening equipment to dig a hole underneath the dome, when there isn't a guard present of course. It's much easier when both of us are there because one of us can always keep lookout and the digging gets done quicker.

I nod but don't feel reassured. It feels as if we are never going to get out and this is the way we are going to live until we all drop dead one by one.

"I'm going to take a shower. Will you grab me some lunch if the guards arrive?"

"Yeah," I say, nodding.

George grins slightly and pats me on the shoulder. I watch him head down towards the far end of the room, through the right-hand open doorway into the shower room.

Chapter 2

I feel sorry for Elliott, I think to myself, as I step into the shower room and begin to undress. I'm keeping my eye on him as he heads over to sit in between Marcus and Harry on one of the benches, but then realises to himself that he isn't going to get any conversation out of either of them seeing as Harry is reading a novel, as always, and Marcus never speaks a word to anyone, so he stands up and crosses the floor to the bench opposite where he takes a place between Mohammed, who likes to talk a lot, and William, who likes to listen a lot. They talk and listen probably for the same reasons as Elliott: to make sure they are still sane, although most of Elliott's talking is inside his own head.

He is just over six feet tall, his hair is short and black, he only shaves once every two to three weeks so most of the time he has a dark beard slowly growing, and he is as muscly as anyone can be on the poor diet we live on as he does his own physical routine every morning: one hundred press-ups, two hundred sit-ups and fifty pull-ups on the bar in the shower room which is fitted to the left-hand open doorway.

He lost his family in the war, all four of them: his wife and his three children; completely wiped out and gone forever, nothing but specks of ash which joined the sky with the rest of the victims.

I slice a thin layer from the end of my bar of soap by using a butter knife I had stolen some months ago when we had been given buttered bread with soup as a treat for dinner when it had been Christmas. No one wanted to think about Christmas, same as the year before, there was nothing to celebrate; the world was fucked and everyone you loved was dead. They wouldn't have known I had stolen it, the guards don't do any checks or searches here, there's no point, life is shit and they couldn't care what we get up to, as long as we stay inside. Besides, things here always go missing; the exact reason why my bar of soap, which everyone receives at the beginning of every third month which must last you the next three, always stays in my pocket, although I have another two underneath my pillow on my bed.

I've become friendly with a guard seeing as we used to go to school together, things like that matter more now in a world where most people you knew are dead, and he sometimes gives me an extra benefit than the others, but I have to keep it quiet otherwise if the others find my contraband it will suddenly be stolen and I'll probably receive threats, the guard will too for favouring me over others, or I'll be accused of being a spy.

The slice I have cut is so thin the light almost passes through it, even though it's a thick pink colouring. The water is cold but manageable; it's either a cold shower or no shower, and after a while, you start to notice the difference in your body such as the reek of onions under your armpits, and although none of us have smelled an onion for years, it's a smell better forgotten when it's leaking from your pores, also not to mention the dirt that collects under your fingernails and toenails due to the dreadful conditions we all live under and especially if you have been gardening, and let's not describe the collection of infectious smegma and aroma from under the foreskin.

I'm used to cold showers and living life a little dirty anyway, seeing as the last world had been full of poor people. I was poor, but not poor-poor, those were really the only classes other than rich and rich-rich. There had been no working class because most people hadn't worked and there had been no middle class because they all became rich by the 2040s. Elliott had been poor too, almost everyone in here had been, with the exception of a couple who had been poor-poor and are thankful to be alive because the conditions here are better than their previous lives. When 'The Bomb' happened the very poor had nothing to lose apart from loved ones, which of course were the most important thing, but the very rich had everything to lose, not including their loves ones.

I begin to scrub underneath my armpits with a frayed sponge, working the soapy iced-water into the creases of my skin as I look down at my body which is now slim. Before the war, before this true starvation, sure, I had been poor, but I had had some meat on me, my belly used to protrude out if I had been wearing a t-shirt slightly too tight for me.

My thoughts then return to Elliott. I then think of his family and how horrible it must have been for him, how horrible it still must be. He never really talks about them, it was only when we first met here, after we had all been herded like sheep and penned inside this shithole, that he told me his family had all died, but he has never told me how he managed to survive if they all died, and I've never asked apart from the first time he spoke of it, but when I had said, "Where were you?" he went silent.

I then begin to think just how little I really know about him and how many other secrets he could be harbouring. Everyone here has past lives in a different world, everyone has stories to tell and probably things to keep to themselves. No one really knows each other that well, no one really has any friends here, we get along with one another as best as we can because we have no choice, we live together so it's silently agreed that we must cope with each other's company to make it easier for everyone.

We are all wary of each other. No one trusts anyone. Some even believe that there could be a spy or two among us working for the guards or the police or the Government or for whoever is in charge now. For what reason? Some say for sociological studies, others argue for historical records, and even some believe there are spies who are here just to make sure that none of us are planning an escape, although an escape seems impossible and even pointless.

Although I myself have an escape plan. I believe it's possible, and it may be pointless, but living here is no way of life. I want to see what's left of the world, just like everyone, we're all constantly imagining how the world looks now and what the future maps will be drawn like. It's the only beautiful image I have, others have memories of their loved ones whereas I had no one before and I have no one now.

Elliott knows of the escape plan of course, we have been working on it together. I don't trust him and I know he doesn't trust me, but we both know that we'll need the assistance of someone else if we want a chance of getting out of here. He doesn't know about the guard giving me handouts though, for some reason it seems important to me that he doesn't have any knowledge of it. Do I suspect he could be the spy? Like I said, no one really trusts anyone here.

The shower stops automatically as they're on a five minute timer. Once the used shower stops the water won't run again for another half-hour. I begin an attempt at drying myself with my towel which is soaking wet because the guards take them away for drying only one day a week, which is another three days away yet.

I start to think of how the escape plan has been so well executed and how we haven't been caught. I then think of how soon it may be coming that Elliott and myself leave this place and all these people behind, it may sound selfish but everyone is to their own devices. You are not responsible for anyone apart from yourself. You have to take care of number one if you don't want to suffer any further or end up dying.

The thought makes me smile as I wrap the towel round my shivering, pimpled body, and I'm caught by surprise when John walks past me, heading towards the toilet room, startling me as he notices my smile which I all of a sudden erase as if I had been hiding something, as if he had read my thoughts and knew of my escape and where the hole was and when I was going to leave.

He closes the toilet room door behind him and I curse myself silently, angry at myself for letting another person see me smile, he would have known I had been thinking about something and it couldn't have been my family like all the others because I never had any family.

You never smile, that's a rule. There's nothing to smile about anymore.

Chapter 3

John was unaware that he was being followed into the toilet room by a lurking presence as he headed towards the far cubicle to release his bladder; it was surprisingly the most desperate he had needed to urinate in a long time, possibly to do with the fact that he had found a flask containing old tea that nobody had discovered and he had drank it all without telling anyone. He knew it must have belonged to Paulo who had recently been rushed out of there because he had become very sick. The guards had informed them that Paulo had had radioactivity related health issues and had died. Everyone had thought of him for only a few seconds and then returned to doing whatever they had been doing. Death was not a shock anymore.

I'd better not let anyone know I stole a dead man's drink, thought John, on his way to the cubicle.

Although he was going to the toilet to urinate, he chose against using the urinal and instead felt he needed to hide himself in private inside the cubicle when doing his business, this time anyway, because if anyone else entered and saw how much he was urinating they may question how he had so much fluid to release.

He was a man of God and peace, and a believer of the human spirit, but when it came down to it, everyone had to do what they had to do and so, knowing that this was true, he accepted his actions.

Nick went past the showers, glancing at George, aware of his presence, as he made sure no one else was going to use the toilet room.

John came to the third cubicle, the cubicle at the end, completely oblivious that the door to the toilet room had opened gently behind him.

All of a sudden he was sent flying inside the cubicle, losing his feet and meeting the tiled wall with his head, sending a buzzing through his ears and blurring his vision briefly. Two hands grabbed him by the collar, pinching his skin in the process, and pulled him back in a shaking manner, treating him like a ragged doll.

"I saw what you did!" came a barking whisper behind his right ear as the intruder locked the cubicle door and gripped the back of his neck with one hand, squeezing gently, almost as if checking his pulse, causing the veins to surface to the skin and bulge like hot, ballooned rivers of blood.

It was Nick, John knew that.

Nick had taken a disliking to him which he was aware of.

"What?" replied John, trying to act innocent but not being at all convincing in his timid voice.

"You drank that dead guy's drink!"

Nick wasn't angry with John because he had drank a drink that had belonged to a dead guy, but instead he was angry with him because he hadn't given him any.

"You think you're more important than the rest of us? You think you're a priority? Well, this is what happens to people like you!"

He wouldn't speak like this or dare do this to anyone else, thought John, *he has been waiting all day for an excuse to pick on me once again.*

Nick bent John over so roughly that John was worried for a moment he had broken his neck, and then pushed him to the ground so John was on his knees, his glasses falling into the toilet. Nick then forced his head inside the bowl of the toilet and pulled the flush, now using both hands to keep him down as John struggled, kicking his legs out and waving his arms around, tapping on the sides of the cubicle, but it was no good, Nick was much stronger.

John felt as if he were drowning as the water swirled all around him, his head being a sinking submarine with holes. He swallowed some of the water and the dirtiness of it began to burn his eyeballs. All of a sudden his trousers became wet too.

I've wet myself, he thought. At least it made Nick release him.

"You've pissed yourself!" cried Nick, standing up with disgust on his face, peering down at the urine that flowed from John's trousers and formed a puddle around his feet.

John was leaning over, his hands over his head, praying to himself that he would not receive any more punishment and humiliation, as he coughed up a portion of toilet water and gasped for his own breath.

"You were desperate. I wonder why," said Nick accusingly.

He turned his back on John who was like a weak animal that couldn't defend itself against the predator, back in the day when there had been animals, and he opened the cubicle door to wash his hands in the sink.

John got to his feet, studied his own urine on the floor in shame as his hair dripped water down his shirt. He retrieved his glasses which were slightly damaged from being beaten up by the water and being blocked at the bottom of the toilet when Nick had flushed it, then put them back on his face after wiping the lenses, and he hurriedly dashed towards the door, leaving with his clothes soaking wet and dripping everywhere, passing Nick with fear and praying that he wouldn't be noticed.

"Yeah, go on! Fuck off!" snapped Nick, laughing to himself and returning his attention to washing his hands.

Harry entered the room, taking a second look at John with his wet clothes and trembling body as he passed him, then seeing Nick at the sink washing his hands.

Nick suddenly became nervous that Harry had seen what had happened. Harry was the biggest guy in The Vault and was worryingly quiet, nobody knew what he was capable of.

He threw a suspicious glance at Nick as he walked by to use one of the urinals, Nick nodded with a weak smile.

There was an awkward pause until Nick spoke, "He just drank Paulo's tea without sharing it with anyone. What a fucking joke, right?"

Harry turned his head over his shoulder slightly, almost peering from the corner of his eye at Nick in the mirror.

"I would have done the same," he said with his strong Scottish accent.

Their eyes met in silence for a few seconds.

Nick shuddered, knowing that Harry hadn't simply been making a statement and been honest, indicating that everyone here would have done the same, even Nick, but instead he had simply been asking Nick if he would have received the same treatment that John had to endure and if Nick would have had the balls to try anything like that with him.

Nick didn't use the half-broken dryer, instead he wiped his hands in his trousers as he scurried out of the toilet room, almost slipping on the stream of John's urine that was now running across the floor.

Chapter 4

"Do you think we're ever getting out of here, Bill?" I ask him, keeping my voice low.

"No I don't, Elliott," the old man replies bluntly and confidently, shaking his head with sad eyes. William, or Bill as some of us choose to call him, is the oldest of us all at the age of seventy-two. He is short and has wild, white hair, the wrinkles in his skin have become more prominent over the last year, and he is the only one who wears his jacket all the time, but he has a reason for this.

"So we're just going to wait until we get ill and die or until we can't take it no longer and top ourselves, like all the others?" I ask, a little bitter from his negative response. I know it's hypocritical of me because I'm always negative, but I don't appreciate his honesty. He has had the same attitude and outlook from day one in The Vault.

"Elliott…" he begins with his croaky, polite tone, "you may have a chance to break out of here if that's what you want, you're younger and stronger, but I'm too old to put up a fight now."

"I'm not planning on breaking out of here…" I start to say, denying that I have a plan.

"Elliott…" Bill chuckles lightly, turning to me on the bench, then looking round to make sure no one is watching or listening, and then returning to my gaze as I watch his lips move slowly with the words quietly slipping from his tired tongue, "everyone here has a plan. Everyone but me. I may be old but I'm not stupid." He smiles. "Just listen to me though. If you manage to get away from here, I will say farewell and wish you good luck, but I think you'll find that when you get out there…" he pauses, raising his right withering hand, pointing a finger at me, "*if* you get out there, I think you'll find there's nothing to embrace, it's all gone. That's what everyone here seems to forget. It's pointless running away from the only life there is to offer, and that life is here."

He turns again to face forward on the bench as I lean back with my head against the cold wall, silently replaying his words in my head.

Everyone here has a plan.

That is very true. You don't know the characters you live among. Is anyone planning a murder? Is anyone planning a suicide? Is the spy planning on handing someone over?

Changing my thought, I then ask myself: *Who is going to drop dead next with pneumonia or radiation poisoning or starvation-related health issues?*

"Paulo was the ninth, right?" I ask, leaning over slightly towards Bill.

"One...two...three..." he counts to himself, the numbers only gently blowing out between his lips as wisps of air. He pauses, I watch his line of thought as he gazes somewhere in the corner of the room. "Yeah," he says, turning to me on his crinkly neck, "he was the ninth to die from his health."

I nod and lean back again to think about Paulo and the other eight before him. Then I begin to think of the seven suicides we've had in the two years in The Vault. The first one had been on the first day of arriving here, a man called Chris, couldn't accept that his family were dead and that the world in many ways had ended, so the following morning we'd found him hanging from the bar that is fitted in the left-hand open doorway from the main room to the shower room, it's where I do my pull-ups every morning, after a while it had left my mind that I was exercising where a man once hung himself using the sheet from his bed.

Two days after he had died, another guy did exactly the same thing, he hung himself on the same bar using his bed sheet. I forgot his name.

Then my thoughts are with the two murders we've had since being there. The first one occurred about a month into our arrival here. This one guy, young and aggressive, had sharpened his toothbrush into a knife-shaped tool and had stabbed a guard in the throat when he had come in to bring our lunch. He bled to death within minutes and the guy that was responsible was taken away and never seen again. After that incident they took away toothbrushes, razors for shaving, and glasses for drinking from, which is why we now only receive them separately and during random periods for a short time, and also why we have to drink from the taps. None of us have ever forgiven him for that.

The other murder happened during one night about four months ago. In the morning, we had discovered this man, who was quite a likeable person I must add, in his bed, not breathing. Someone in the night had smothered him with a pillow. Nobody owned up to it. Nobody claimed to have seen or heard anything. The guards questioned each one of us but they had no information. The body was taken away and it was never talked about again. Someone here did it and there must have been a witness, or witnesses. I didn't have any involvement and nor do I know of anything that happened that night, apart from the fact that the man who had been killed had had an argument with Nick the night before over whose turn it was to use one of the chairs in the playroom, and everyone knew about this argument because we had all heard it, but nobody repeated anything about it since.

I think about the three people that had been taken away by the guards without any reason. The first had been about three months in, the second had been after a year and the third had been about after a year and two months. All of them must have had escape plans and had been grassed to the guards by the spy. There is a spy here, I'm certain. For all I know it could be Bill sat next to me right now, which is why you never give away any information to anyone.

I then begin to think about Ali. He had been around his mid-twenties, always kept himself to himself and had put on an act for the first three months that he was stupid. He was the last person you would have expected to manage to escape.

Following the morning of his bed being found empty it was discovered that he had locked himself inside the middle cubicle of the toilet room sometime during the night and had used some kind of tool to lift up a square section of tiles on the floor which led to the piping which he had crawled through. He was never seen again, but everyone remembers his name.

It is unclear as to whether he ever managed to escape or if it had been a failed attempt. We are unsure whether he got himself stuck halfway down a pipe and suffocated to death or whether the guards had caught him and possibly took him to another vault or maybe even killed him. But when any of us talk of him we always imagine he escaped The Vault and somehow got himself to the other side of the dome and ran away into the hills with his freedom.

"Jerry won't be joining that list though," comes Bill's voice, knocking me out from my daydream.

"Huh?" I say, turning to see that he is stroking the head of Jerry, his pet rat, poking its head out from his inside jacket pocket—the reason Bill always wears it, it's the rat's home.

"Dying. Jerry won't be one of them," he says. "Rats can sense things that we can't."

Everyone knows he owns the rat, apart from the guards which would see it as a health hazard. None of us think it matters, apart from a couple that have a problem with being around rats, but there are enough rats here among us anyway, and I'm not talking about the type that is in Bill's pocket.

"When is lunch going to arrive?" comes another voice.

I turn over my other shoulder to face Mohammed who is sitting to my right. He is about thirty, is clean shaven every Monday morning, and he keeps his hair short whenever the haircuts are offered. He is friendly but is also known to be someone who doesn't mind his own business, some have even accused him of being the spy.

He is pointing at the lights above The Door. It's the door that is locked twenty-four hours a day apart from when the guards enter. Above The Door there are two light bulbs behind a caged box. One of the lights is red and the other is green. The red one burns almost every second of the day until The Door is unlocked when the guards are entering, then the red light dies and the green light comes on, that's our signal for food, and it's almost what we use as a clock. When it comes on and they enter the first time in the day, we know that it's midday as lunch arrives; when it turns on the second time of the day and the guards enter with our second meal, we know it's early evening.

I stare at the red light and then speak with my back to Mohammed, "I don't know, but I hope it's soon."

We wait for lunch to arrive without talking much, Bill to my left and Mohammed to my right, sat upright on the bench with our backs and heads resting against the wall, and our legs stretched out.

It is only then that I notice John, the religious-peace-hippy guy with his long, scraggly hair and his glasses, is sat on the bench in the middle of the room, opposite myself. He has returned from going to the toilet but is drenched in water and has a look of despair on his face. I like John, so do most people. He may talk a lot, he may preach a lot and he may be the number one theorist, but he means well and wouldn't harm anyone.

Seconds later, I watch Nick, the slightly ugly, fierce-looking guy who feels the need to project a masculine appearance and prove himself at all times, return from the toilet room as well and sit on the other side of Bill, throwing John a glance.

The light is still red.

Then Harry comes back from the toilet room and takes his place on the edge of the middle bench, closest to The Door so he'll be first to get his hands on the food when it finally arrives, and keeping a little distance between himself and John.

Harry, the big Scottish guy, is about six-five in height, he is in his fifties with a good set of hair still left, turning grey over time, and he exercises daily like myself, but he is able to produce three times the amount of work than me which is why his arms are like tree trunks. He rarely speaks to anyone unless they speak to him first and he spends all his time every single day with his nose in one of the books from one of the bookcases in the playroom. He must have read a hundred books since being here. One rule we have here is that you do not disturb Harry when he is reading, which is basically all the time, so just don't disturb Harry, leave him to himself.

Harry takes the book he had been reading before going to the toilet out from his trousers where he tucked it and returns to reading. The fact that he had taken his book to the toilet with him proves that either he can't bear to be without it or he doesn't trust anyone to not pick it up and decide they want to start reading it.

Not that anyone would dare pick up a book he is reading. Nobody asks him what he's reading or what it's about or if it's any good. No one cares to be honest, but it's more to do with what I said before, the rule we have: you do not disturb Harry when he is reading.

Chapter 5

I read so everyone leaves me alone. Don't get me wrong, I enjoy reading, but I don't read now because of pure enjoyment. I do it so nobody talks to me, so I can lose myself and pretend I don't live here among these people I have no interest in, and more so because in the last month I have been finding messages. Messages within the books. Someone keeps leaving these messages and they're directed at me.

I don't know what the point of the messages are or why they're being left for me to discover and solve, or even who it is that keeps writing them, but it keeps me going, almost like a game. Someone here, one of the other fifteen guys I live with, wants to talk to me in private about something.

I look up to the red light above The Door and sigh. Fuck me, I'm hungry. Before returning to my book I catch a glimpse of Elliott staring at me, we lock eyes for a second before he feels intimidated and looks the other way. He's an alright guy, a little sad in the eyes for my liking, but he's alright.

Myself, I've not accepted what's happened, but I understand better than the rest of them. Humans fucked up. Again. The world has, in many ways, ended. But it's not all bad. I see positives in the world we now live in. For example: there is no currency, there are no classes and we are all equal.

It's true that the days of enjoying a nice meal, even though I had been poor beforehand so I had only had one *nice* meal a week anyway, and the days even before the war, even farther back, before 2055, when you could enjoy some pleasant sex, are long gone. You don't get used to this life and you don't accept it. If anyone here says they have either gotten used to it or accepted it, then they're either lying or insane.

But putting all of that behind you, you have to ask yourself: Now what? Work forward, put up a fight and keep on living. And

I, like everyone else here, have a plan. I'm getting out of here once I get an opportunity. And I believe that that opportunity is within the hidden messages I keep finding. First of all I just need to figure them out.

I pretend to read the small, rectangular, green cover book in my large hands, hands which were once used for boxing when I was a young man and when the world was a different place, and I stare at the message in the top left corner of the page which reads, in black ink: *OEbyPWpg245*.

I know what it means. This is the third message I have received. The first one had been in a copy of *War of the Worlds* that I had been reading, on the first page: **Harry, read some Dickens.**

Mohammed was the one that had recommended me to read *War of the Worlds* so I initially thought he had written the message inside, but he denied any knowledge of it. I hadn't told him I had received a message obviously, I just asked him if there was anything he wanted to tell me. I didn't want him knowing. He was the nosiest person here and he would have probably followed the messages to figure it out before me; I trust him least of all, he is too friendly and talkative.

I peer over my book and glance at him. I believe he is a spy working for the guards. I'm spying on the spy, trying to decipher him.

After I had received the first message I searched for books, on the shelves of the bookcases, by Charles Dickens, and there were two: *Oliver Twist* and *David Copperfield.*

I read *Oliver* back to back and found nothing so then read *Copperfield* and had found a message on the twentieth-something page that read: **GrnCovrBrkSpnBck**.

It took me two days to work out that it meant: Green Cover, Broken Spine, Back. So I found the only book with a green cover and a broken spine and turned to the back page where there was a sketch of a fish, as if it were a joke from the messenger: I am the fish and he, whoever he is, is trying to hook me and reel me in. In the middle of the fish's eye was the number **91** written. At first, I thought I had to find a book called 91, then I thought maybe the books were categorised by number and it was the 91st on the shelf, but luckily I decided that maybe it was just a clue for the actual message which could be in the same book, so I turned to page 91 which is what I stare at now.

I'm going to act after I eat, but I don't stop pretending to read otherwise everyone will know something is different, so I turn the page to hide the message from anyone walking past or maybe leaning over, and then sneakily twitch my eyes round the room to see who may be the master behind the messages.

There's John, two spaces from me, but the poor guy isn't capable of looking after himself, let alone capable of trying to forge a plan. Then there's George just entering the room after taking a shower as he sits to the right of John and nearer to me, he gives a look to Elliott who looks back, but neither of them say anything, they're talking with their mouths shut, they're sharing a thought. The two of them are always talking, always together, I know that they're planning something, but I have no interest in their plan, I'm interested in mine. Neither of them would dare let anyone else in on their plan, so it's neither of them that are sending the messages.

I lean forward slightly and notice Marcus, sat by himself as usual, on the other end of the bench, to John's left, staring into space and biting his fingernails, exposing the scars on his hands. It seems like new cuts appear on his palms every day, I'm sure others have noticed. I believe he's about nineteen, the youngest of us, he hasn't spoken a word since coming here, in two years he has remained silent. He definitely isn't the culprit, not to be horrible but the kid is most definitely unintelligible, he's in his own world and has probably lost his mind.

Opposite me, sat on the right of Elliott (his left), is the old guy Bill. He doesn't care about anything but staying alive in this place until his time is up and trying to convince us that this is the only life available to us, other than that he only cares about that bloody rat he keeps in his pocket. Then next to him is that real asshole, Nick. If it is him contacting me, then I will lose all faith. There's Kris, who likes magic tricks, the two old fellas that play cards with him daily, Hal and Roger, they're in the playroom at this moment, and there's Steve, Yung-Lee, Marcus (who is known as Mark in order not to confuse him with the other Marcus), Samuel and Ben, all of whom are in the bedroom at this moment, and all of whom never spend enough time around me to even remember my name.

I guess I'll have to wait for him to show himself. I'll go find the next book, the next message, after I eat. Hopefully I'll be closer to revealing his identity.

There's a buzz in the corner of my ear and everyone sat in the main room looks up before the three from the playroom and the five from the bedroom all come rushing in, as I notice that the green lightbulb has turned on and The Door is being unlocked.

Chapter 6

As the two armed guards in military uniforms entered, one of them pushing a trolley ahead of them which supplied food and flasks, the other standing behind to prevent anyone from attacking or attempting to flee, John was the only one that didn't get to his feet.

Instead he allowed everyone to rush forward to retrieve their paper plates which served one dry bread roll each with a thin spread of butter inside and their flasks that had been newly filled, a quarter of the way, with warm tea. He also allowed them to fight for their way back to a bench to sit and scoff their food as quickly as they possibly could, knocking into each other, pushing, pulling, shoving, and swearing.

The sounds of pleasurable sighs from the consumption of food for the first time in about eighteen hours, the groans and desperate bites, the rapid chewing and swallowing where none of them really gave time to taste what they were eating, the rumbling stomachs and slurping lips, all these noises echoed around the main room as John stood there watching.

He finally got to his feet and headed over to the trolley to place the last bread roll on a paper plate and to collect his flask before he walked back to the bench to find that Nick was sat there in his place, looking up at him whilst pushing the last mouthful of his roll into his smirking mouth.

John didn't bother saying anything, instead he walked past him and stood round the corner of the centre bench, nearer the windows, as he shivered slightly from his head still being wet.

"Thank you God for this food…" he whispered to himself as he raised the bread roll to his mouth to take a bite, his eyes not leaving the butter that had oozed out the side in such a splendid stream, he could already taste it.

"Now now…" said Nick, now standing in front of him, distracting him from his meal and causing him to freeze with the roll inches from his tongue. "You're going to save that for me, is that right? You weren't thinking of eating all of that by yourself, were you?"

Nick snatched the roll from John's weak hand and slyly slipped it into his trouser pocket. John's eyes were now those of a child who had had their favourite toy broken.

No one else was paying any attention to the two of them standing near the windows as their concentration was so focused on their own food and the chaos that the arrival of any food within those walls caused.

"I'll keep it safe for you," whispered Nick, inches from John's face, his warm breath smothering him with the scent of bread as if teasing him. "And you won't need this seeing as you have already helped yourself to someone else's today."

Nick bent over and picked up John's flask that he had placed between his feet whilst he was about to eat, and then unscrewed the lid which was a cup that was used to pour the tea into. Nick didn't bother with the cup and put the flask to his lips, tilted his head back and drank every last drop before slapping his tongue about his mouth, burping in John's face and wiping his lips with the back of his hand, never removing his eye contact from John's defeated face.

Nick handed John the flask which he took with a feeble grip, and smiled at him, waiting to see what he would do. What could he do? He was standing there with an empty flask and a paper plate that contained nothing more than a few bread crumbs, and his stomach so badly ached from hunger to the point that he felt sick. Everyone felt sick most of the time, especially after eating because it was such a shock to the body.

"Has anyone not received their food or drink?" called the first guard, the one that had pushed the trolley in. His name was Anthony, he was tall, had short hair and a very sharp face. None of those in The Vault liked him.

"You say anything and I'll make sure you never eat again," whispered Nick in John's ear, now standing beside him, the bread roll in his pocket almost rubbing against John's leg as if teasing him even more.

Nick bent John's hand, the one which was holding the paper plate, behind his back, arching his wrist. If he bent it any further, John was sure it would break. His bones weren't strong.

Nobody said anything. There was a pause as they watched the guards eyeballing the room, examining each individual as if to read their minds.

"Right. In that case, I have mail for Number 634," said Anthony.

Samuel stood up and everyone watched him approach the guard. Everyone then looked at his brown envelope which he carried back to his bench, wondering who it was from, where it had come from, what it said, why he had received one and they hadn't, and studying his facial expressions as he read it.

He was twenty-five years old, shaved rarely, had a full head of blonde hair, and spent most of his time relaxing on his bed either reading or talking to himself.

"It's from my sister," he said aloud to himself and unintentionally to everyone else, causing every head to turn. "She's alive and she found my name on the list!" A tear ran down his cheek before he walked to the bedroom with the letter held out in front of him with both thumbs and index fingers, not looking where he was going, and continuing to talk to himself.

"And there is mail for Number 649," said Anthony.

Chapter 7

My mouth gaped open as I cast a stern look at Elliott.

Who's that from? I ask silently, only with thought.

I don't know George, he replies without speaking but with a shrug of the shoulders.

Can I trust him? I ask myself, again. *No, but I need him.*

Elliott gets to his feet and approaches the guard, snatching the envelope from his hand, and then heads to the playroom without taking his eyes from the letter, avoiding everyone.

"That's the only mail," says Anthony in the background as I continue to stare in the direction of the open doorway to the playroom where Elliott is now inside, by himself, alone with that envelope. I'm not jealous that he has received one and I haven't, I am curious as to who it is from. His entire family had died during the war, so who could there be alive that knows him and recognised his name on the list? Unless there is a distant relative or possibly a friend, either way he has no knowledge of them being alive because he has never mentioned anything, and he has never sent a letter himself so this would all be new to him…

Hold on, I pause my thought. *How do I know he hasn't sent a letter before? Why would he tell me?*

It's none of my business but you can't help wanting to know if someone else has a secret, especially if it's the person you spend most of your time with.

I try to reassure myself that someone could have mistaken his name on the list for someone they used to know, but not knowing for sure is making me paranoid, it's scratching away at the back of my mind, asking questions. It is also always suspicious when someone receives a letter, as it happens so infrequently, and a lot of us wonder whether the person receiving the letter is in fact a spy. Elliott and Samuel will both have eyes kept on them all day today; they'll be followed to whichever room they go to, they'll be eavesdropped when they go to the toilet and when they go to bed, they'll have every one of their facial muscles studied, and if they're caught staring out of a window for longer than usual, then people will begin believing that they've been offered a deal by the guards, maybe to return information on others or any plans they know of in return for luxuries or even their freedom? Again, this is all speculation and theories.

"And…" the guard continues, as I remain staring at the doorway to the playroom, picturing my eyes stretching out so far that they manage to peep round the corner and see if Elliott is reading the letter, or even, my eyes manage to read the letter, so my brain can secretly store the information for me to access when I want, "Lucas has the list for garden duty," says Anthony, turning slightly to the other guard, Lucas, behind him, standing closer to The Door, pulling out a sheet of paper from inside his uniform pocket.

Lucas is stocky, multiracial and too friendly to take seriously. He also happens to be the guard I sometimes manage to get things passed under the table from.

"Garden duty today will be Numbers 637 (John), 641 (Ben) and 645 (me). So if you three would like to get ready," he says, only looking in my direction, "then we can get going in a couple of minutes."

Isn't that a surprise? I had put my name down, along with ten others, and I had managed to get chosen, but it doesn't work every time. If Lucas had allowed me to garden every time, it would become clear that there was a case of favouritism going on.

"Next garden duty will be in two days' time so if anyone would like to sign up, come over to me now so I can put your name down on the list," says Lucas.

I wait for the others that are putting their names down to return to their benches before I approach Lucas to sign Elliott and me up for garden duty, just like I do every time, to ensure that the hole we have been digging for the last four months will be dug quicker, so we can leave here sooner.

"Make sure that Elliott, that's Number 649, and me, both get priority in two days' time. If you do that, then I won't ask for any favours for a month, and that's a promise," I whisper to Lucas, whilst Anthony collects the empty paper plates and stacks them on top of the trolley.

If we are given priority for garden duty in two days' time, then I will never ask for another favour from Lucas ever again because I'll be gone. I am going to make sure that the hole is completely dug today and is ready for Elliott and me to leave through in two days.

Lucas stares at me, nods and adds Elliott's name to the list, underneath mine.

John and Ben join me at The Door with Lucas; we allow Anthony to pass through with the trolley who leads the three of us out into the hallway, before Lucas closes The Door and locks it.

Chapter 8

When I said that everyone I had known is dead, that was a slight lie. And when I said I have never received a letter before, other than the one I have now, that was also a lie.

I had received a letter about a month ago, the only other one I have ever received. It was from the same person as the one I hold now. The mail that day, a month ago, had arrived a little later than usual. Half-hour after lunch the guards had returned to The Vault with two letters, one of which was for me, the other I can't remember who it was for, I wasn't paying attention. Luckily that day George had been out on garden duty, so he had no knowledge of me ever receiving one.

He had even asked me when returning that day, "I heard the mail was late. Didn't get a letter, did you?" in a joking manner. I had laughed and told him that I had not.

The reason I didn't want George knowing about the first letter was because he would have asked about it and I would have had to tell him. Now that this letter had arrived, it was a little different, he was there, he heard my number being called out and he saw me receive it.

That's why I came in here, to the playroom, to almost hide from everyone, especially George, because he would have tried to read it and ask who it was from.

He's a good guy but he has to know my business, everyone here wants to know each other's business, because our lives are so boring and uninteresting, because we want to know if anyone is planning to escape and because no one can trust each other. Luckily for me, George is out on garden duty again today, so I have some time to myself to be able to read it and to think about what I am going to do.

The letter is from someone I knew before the war. Her name is Jane and she lives in the vault, which is, the top floor of the building opposite the window at the back of the playroom, where I stand right now, looking out through the glass and the caged bars and into the vault where women live.

The letter she had sent me a month ago had simply told me that she was alive and that she was living in the floor opposite mine and that she had seen me. It also confessed that she loved me and had never stopped thinking or crying over me.

I had gone to the window that day and seen her. We smiled, but neither of us could wave or show any sign that we were communicating with someone from another vault, my reason being that people here would know I knew someone, even though most of them, apart from George and a couple of others that may have been on garden duty with him the day I received the letter, would have known that fact anyway, but I didn't want them knowing who it was. I'm not sure if her reasons were the same though; it's quite possible that the way of life and the attitude we have in The Vault isn't the same in others. Maybe they trust each other? Maybe they don't have theories about spies and escape plans? Although many of us have spoken to others from other vaults whilst on garden duty, which is forbidden, and they have shared similar beliefs and outlooks, all I remember is one guy saying he had over fifty men living on his floor, and another guy saying that the guards allowed women to join their floor once a fortnight, but I think both of them had either been lying or just trapped in their own imaginations.

I have been coming to this window every day to see if she is standing there looking back at me. I always try to do it when no one is in the playroom and I do it at different times so nobody begins to notice my routine. The last thing I want is someone knowing that there is a woman I know that lives in the vault opposite ours and that she is the one that is sending me letters.

I sent a letter back, confessing my love and telling her not to send me another for a month or two. The reason for this, other than avoiding making everyone suspicious of me, was to make sure that the hole that George and I had been digging would be ready by then, so the two of us could flee together. The two of us being Jane and I, not George and I. I am letting him think that the hole is going to be dug for us two, but whilst he is out there digging right now, he has no knowledge that, in fact, I am going to be leaving without him.

I have to do what I have to do. No one here is a friend. No one here trusts each other. Everyone will stab anyone in the back for their own freedom.

I am now reading the new letter, the second one from Jane, which reads:

Elliott, my love, I cannot wait to be with you. The wait has been too long. I can't sleep at night until you have me in your arms. We shall be together again soon. I will be on garden duty in two days' time. If this is good for you, then please meet me at the window. Love Jane xxxxx

George had said that he was going to put our names on the list, so that's why I am standing at the window, holding the letter and staring out to her opposite me, returning the smile she sends across. I had heard Lucas confirm that the next duty would be in two days, so that worked out well.

As long as George has done what he said he would, then I have two days to rearrange the plan, the real plan, not the plan that George believes is going to take place and as long as George manages to complete digging the hole. The last time one of us was on garden duty, which was five days ago and had been me, I had noticed that there was only about half a foot of soil remaining when the whistle had been blown, which signalled the guards calling for all gardeners to return to the front doors of their buildings where they would be queued and counted, and would return their gardening equipment before being escorted back to their vaults.

He only has half a foot to dig, he will definitely have it done today, I think to myself and smile. I had heard his number being called out when I had come in here to read my letter and that's why I immediately went to the window to let Jane know that our plan will be taking place soon. It was just lucky that the next garden duty would be in two days.

Suddenly, a horrid thought occurs to me, a thought so extremely terrifying that I have to step away from the window and stare at the letter with pain searing through my heart.

What if George leaves, today, right now, without me? What if he realises that there is only half a foot to dig and that he could just leave by himself? We both know that we only need each

65

other for the digging because it will get done quicker, but once the hole is dug and the soil is gone, we no longer need each other. The open air is out there and he could crawl underneath and run away, leaving me trapped inside here, locked inside The Vault with all the others, in this building, high off the ground, with no air to breathe and nothing real to touch. I know it's exactly what I intend to do to him but the thought of having my own plan used against me is too much of a nightmare to even comprehend.

"That's nice…" comes a voice from behind, startling me. I turn around to see Mohammed standing there, causing me to fold the letter and hold it by my side.

"What?" I ask innocently, as if he has been listening to my thoughts.

"Staring at the women again?" he laughs, pointing out the window to Jane's vault in the opposite building. I turn back to look out again but she has gone, probably startled, too, by Mohammed's appearance.

"What do you mean *again*?" I ask, over-offensively.

"You're always standing here," he says, walking round me with his smarmy grin and his intelligent and curious eyebrows constantly twitching.

"Am I?"

He doesn't reply, just stands there looking at me, trying to look into my eyes to read my thoughts and see what I'm hiding.

It creeps me out and makes me feel uneasy, so I put the letter back inside the envelope and tuck it into my pocket. The first letter I received a month ago I have kept in the bottom of my right shoe the whole time, underneath my foot. If you keep it under your mattress or it accidently falls from your pocket, then someone will steal it, read it and share it. Once I'm out of this room, I will put this letter in my left shoe.

"Don't mind me," says Mohammed, watching me tuck my letter away as I edge for the door, "I'm just coming in here to find a book."

Chapter 9

Elliott leaves through the open doorway and I'm by myself in the playroom. I take a quick peek out of the window he was staring out from, the one which looks directly across to the vault that is level with ours, the one filled with women. I have seen him standing here many times, staring out to that floor, and I know he isn't just looking at the women because he wants something nice to look at or because he pictures having sex with them. All the other guys stopped staring out the window after being here for two weeks, but he continues to stare out of it after two years, although he has only been doing so for the last month. In the last month, he has discovered something, something about the vault in that building. And I remember, unlike anyone else here probably does, that he received a letter about a month ago; it's been since then that you can find him here at random moments, each day, by himself, staring out of the window.

Someone over there has contacted him, I know it. He knows someone over there. The two of them are communicating through letters. They will arrange to meet. They will arrange to escape eventually, just like everyone here plans to. His whole family died in the war though, or so he says, so I'm not sure who the person could be, but I will find out.

I know everyone and everything here and what I don't know, I eventually find out. I'm only nice to everyone in order to gain as much information as I can because I am wary of every single person. The only person here I trust and care about is myself.

I squeeze the penny coin I keep in my pocket, and have kept in my pocket for two years inside The Vault, between two fingers, almost rubbing it. It's the only item I have from my past life, from the past world. I used to carry it with me everywhere for good luck because it was dated the year I was born, then when 'The Bomb' happened and I had survived, I realised it was inside my pocket and it has made me more superstitious than ever. No one knows I have it.

I return my focus to why I have come into the playroom. I am here to find a book. Any book which might give me a clue as to what Harry is really reading so much for. I had recommended *War of the Worlds* to him a while ago, all out of complete innocence, only because I had read it and thought he might like it because he read so often, and since then he has been acting strange, much more quiet than usual, and it is as if he is no longer reading because he enjoys the stories, but it's as if he is trying to get through all of the books in the playroom as quickly as he can, as if there is something in them that can help him escape from here. I am here to try and find out for myself.

I walk round to one of the three bookcases. There is one against the right wall, one against the left wall, and the other one, the one I am at, is between the two of them, in the middle. When you stand on one side of it, the window-side, anyone standing at the door would not know you were behind there. That's where I am standing.

All of a sudden, Harry appears and although he is a heavy guy, when he doesn't want to make himself known, his footsteps are like those of a mouse. He freezes by the window, having purposely turned, intending to come behind the bookcase I am at, to search for his next book, or of course the next hidden message someone may have left him. It's as if I have caught him and he has caught me, the two of us, our eyes locked like two predators preparing to attack, and my hand is resting on the book which his eye now levels with. I raise my eyebrows and peer at the title of the book, wondering what could be written in there for him. It's as if we have come here for the same reason and with the same thought in mind, although he knows what he is looking for, whereas I have coincidentally stumbled upon it.

"You!" Harry growls, taking two striding steps towards me, now making himself known as his gigantic feet cause the floor to vibrate beneath mine and probably cause those living below us to hear, as he reaches out a hand and grabs me round the collar of my shirt (I always wear long sleeves to hide my skinny arms, whereas Harry always wears short sleeves exposing his muscular arms).

"What?" I cry, cowering, putting my hands up in innocence and backing away as he tightens his grip round my collar and shoves me up against the wooden shelves and books.

"You know what!" he barks, spraying saliva over me, but keeping his tone down so no one else overhears from the other room.

"I don't," I lie, looking up to him as he towers above me.

"You know why I've found you here. You're the one sending me the fucking messages. Why? Is it to play a trick on me? Or are you trying to set me up for something? What are they all about?"

"It's not me, Harry," I reply calmly and honestly.

He pauses, glaring at me with rage, and then releases his grip and lets me down before stepping away to calm himself with his hands on his hips.

"I know it's you! How come I've found you here? How come you have your hand on the exact book I'm looking for? You tell me," he whispers, peering a couple of times around the corner of the bookcase to make sure no one else has entered the playroom.

"I don't know what you're talking about," I say, knowing too well what he's talking about, although of course he's wrong about accusing me of being the messenger, "I'm being serious, it isn't me."

Harry grabs the book I had laid my hand on and snatches it from the shelf before tucking it into the back of his trousers and covering it with his t-shirt.

"But now that you've told me, I am intrigued," I say. "Once you've finished reading that, you wouldn't mind passing it onto me, would you?"

Harry turns on his heels, his face lowered but his eyes not leaving me. He is reading my smirk and how my eyes have lit up with interest.

"What messages?" I ask.

"Never mind," Harry sighs. "Just mind your own business."

"I find that hard to accept. Good luck though." I watch him turn away, about to leave, and then I say, "If you find out who they're from then let me know, unless of course I find out before you." He stands still, his back to me. "Which is highly likely."

Chapter 10

I walk away from Mohammed and leave the playroom, walk past everyone in the main room and head straight for the bedroom.

Inside the bedroom there are sixteen beds, eight either side of the room, all in line with one another. It is displayed like an old army camp or a prison camp. My bed is the third from the far wall on the right-hand side. There used to be many more beds when there had been more of us, they had been all crammed side by side, you were literally holding hands when you went to sleep, there even used to be beds in the main room when we first arrived, but now there are less people and a lot more space. The beds are all wooden, the sheets and pillows are all white, there is one wooden shelf above each bed for people to keep their own bars of soap and cigarettes and whatever on, and the walls in this room are a dark greyish-blue.

There is no one else in here, everyone else is in the main room or taking showers. I take the book I had been reading from under my t-shirt and tuck it under my mattress for now. I had been about to put it back on the bookcase and collect my next one, but after having found Mohammed there I decided it would be best to keep it too, just so he wouldn't start reading it to find my message and try to follow whatever it was I was following, which he sure as hell would have done.

I remove the other book, the new one, from the back of my trousers and then lie down on my bed, glad to be away from everyone so I can read my message in private.

The message I had received and had figured out before lunch had read: *OEbyPWpg245*.

The book I had picked up, the one which that sly bastard Mohammed had had his hands on and was probably about to open, is called: *Only Emeralds* and it is by *Patricia Williams* (it had been released in 2036 and was a modern classic but had also been one of the last novels to have been written and published for the average person to afford, I had read it when I was younger and thought it was incredible), I turn to page 245.

Someone enters the bedroom and I try not to make it obvious that I have discovered something new, I just pretend I'm reading.

I roll my head on the pillow and notice it's Elliott that has come in. He glances at me with an effort to smile, which I do not return but instead continue to study him with wariness, and then he flops himself down on his bed which is on my row, the seventh from the far wall, so he's second closest to the doorway on this side of the room, and he lays there with one hand under his head, staring up at the ceiling.

I return my attention to the book. On page 245, which is where I was informed to locate myself, there is a sentence that has been underlined in the same black ink which reads: ***There was dust collecting on the shelf***.

I whisper the sentence to myself two or three times whilst staring at it. Then I look up to think and whisper it several more times but not aloud in case anyone sees me thinking or speaking to myself, or if Elliott thinks I'm talking to him and realises I'm not reading my book then it'll look odd, or if the guards have cameras and microphones here and realise I am thinking about something I have read.

There was dust collecting on the shelf, I whisper in my head, reciting the sentence from the book that has been underlined. What kind of clue is that? Is that even a message? What does it mean?

I close the book and tuck it underneath my mattress with the other one and then lie there with my hands crossed over my stomach as I close my eyes and repeat the sentence over and over in my head.

If anyone sees me like this, they'll assume I'm sleeping or just resting, none of them will know that I am in fact thinking and figuring and planning.

After a minute or two passes I open my eyes and breathe out gently, no further and no more successful than I had been before closing my eyes in working out the message.

Suddenly…

71

Meet 2nd cubicle when you find this. I will know to follow. Bring book.

It appears in front of me, written in black ink on the underneath of my shelf that is above my bed as I stare up at it in disbelief, and there is dust collecting on the shelf, that's true. Someone has written this on here for me, I still don't know who, but I think I'm going to find out, they want to arrange a meeting.

If anyone sees me now, they will presume I am relaxing, having no clue that in fact I am still reading. Reading the message that is written on the bottom of my shelf, written in such a hidden place and written so small that you wouldn't see it unless you were lying on my bed, which nobody does but me. The person that wrote the message must have been very clever to have done this, knowing full well that at any moment someone else could have entered the room, even me, and they would have been caught and the message would have been found and there would have been trouble with the guards, or a spy would have reported them, or someone would have told everyone and that person's plan would have been destroyed, meaning my plans would have been destroyed. This person has risked a lot for me. I have to thank him, whoever he is.

I turn my head slightly to see if Elliott has moved. He hasn't. He has now closed his eyes, is possibly even asleep or he could be thinking and planning like I am; that's the way everyone here lives, inside their heads. Our minds are the real vaults.

After rolling over gently, I take the new book from under the mattress, intending to do as the message asks by bringing the book to the arranged meeting, and I stroll out of the bedroom and back into the main room casually.

Before I go to the toilet room and wait for the messenger to meet me, I decide to take a seat on the edge of the bench that is closest to the bedroom doorway and cross my legs, open the book to the fourth page, aware that Mohammed is watching and knows I picked up the book only minutes ago and therefore can't be too far into the story, and then I examine the room.

I can hear the showers are on and I can hear talking from the playroom as people play cards. In the main room, there is Bill sitting two spaces away from me stroking the rat in his pocket, there is Mohammed walking up and down by the windows at a slow pace, now and then glancing at me with that smirk on his face, and there is Marcus sitting on the centre bench opposite me fiddling nervously with the worn fringes of his pockets as he stares down at the ground like a child having been scolded by an adult. Elliott is in the bedroom, and there are three guys out on garden duty.

The messenger is here somewhere. He is waiting for me to make my move by heading to the toilet room to meet him. I have the book in my hands to make it obvious that I have found the next message and to make him aware that the meeting will be happening today. I am putting myself in the main living space to make myself noticed. But who is it?

All of a sudden, there is a click as something strikes the ground. My eyes look up, peering over the book; Bill's eyes briefly glance at what it is on the ground and acknowledges there is contraband but ignores it to return his adoration to his rat. Mohammed is at the far end of the window, he has stopped pacing up and down and is now leaning into the right-hand doorway of the shower room and talking to someone, he hasn't noticed or heard what has just happened.

A pen has fallen onto the ground. A black inked pen. It has fallen from Marcus's pocket.

As a hint or by accident? It doesn't matter. Marcus owns a pen. A black pen.

Nobody here owns pens. Nobody needs pens, nobody is allowed to have sharp objects, but he has one.

He is the messenger. I'm sure of it.

The click it had made as it had struck the floor had made him slightly bolt upright. He bends over quickly as if not wanting anyone to know and tucks it back into his pocket. I follow Marcus's eyes as they scan Bill and then side-scan past him and land on me.

My heart is beating in my throat, I feel the warmest I have felt all my life. My skin is burning; I am eye-to-eye with the person that has been contacting me and it turns out to be the silent, dumb kid.

But he isn't so silent after all. He has spoken out to me, only *in* silence, there's a difference.

And he obviously isn't so dumb after all, nor is he just some kid.

I nod sneakily with the book covering half of my face, trying not to make it obvious to Bill sitting nearby and making sure that Mohammed isn't looking over his shoulder.

I get to my feet, tuck the book into the back of my trousers and cover it with my t-shirt, before heading to the toilet room without trying to show any intention in my walk or my expression, knowing that Mohammed will be watching and timing me, and may possibly follow me or keep an eye on who does.

Chapter 11

They all think I'm dumb or strange because I don't speak. But it's the way I choose to live. It's the wisest way to be if you want to survive here.

As I'm the youngest they have all decided between themselves that I'm just a kid, but I'm a kid that has turned twenty today. Nobody knows this, not only because I haven't told anyone, but even if they had known the date of my birthday they wouldn't have known it was today because none of them pay attention to the date, whereas I have been mentally keeping a calendar since arriving here so I'm aware of what day, month and year it is. They all say it's been two years since being here but if they had been calculating properly like myself then they would know it has been over two years, to be exact it has been seven hundred and forty-one days.

I will be gone by the seven hundred and forty-third day. A lot of people will be gone soon, or will attempt to be gone, because everyone has a plan and it's becoming more and more evident that it is going to take place very shortly. You can sense it when you wake up in the morning, you can sense it during every shower and each meal and every game of cards that's played. They all have their own motives and they're all going to act within a matter of days, that I am sure of.

When you spend all your time by yourself and in complete silence you have the whole time and nothing but the time to just sit and study your surroundings. I know everyone's game. I don't trust a single person here.

Elliott and George are obviously leaving together and their plan is going to take place during garden duty hours seeing as they are always volunteering and it helps that George is obviously friendly with the guard Lucas, they're usually talking privately and his name usually appears on the list, no one seems to have noticed but me.

Nick is looking for any opportunity he can find to be a part of even though he wouldn't be welcome in anyone's plans, he knows this, but he also knows that he can't leave here by himself, he isn't intelligent enough to formulate a plan. John doesn't seem to believe any more bad can happen in the world and that God has chosen us to be the selected survivors so we should appreciate it, and he believes this place is all we have and therefore his plan is to remain here, he wouldn't even dare dream of escaping. Bill doesn't care, he's too old to run away, he's always telling the rest of us that we should stay here, and the same goes for the other two old guys: Hal and Roger. Those two play cards most of the time with Kris, the mysterious magician, almost as if they're waiting for him to come up with a trick that will magically put them on the other side of the dome, that's their only hope. Kris is friendly and gets along with everyone, but he doesn't ever talk about anything apart from cards and he especially doesn't talk about the war or his previous life, his theory is that what's happened has happened, we must adapt to the new way of life. He's the only one that I know that plans to leave by himself, I'm not too sure how, but he definitely has the cogs in his brain working on something. Mohammed has the biggest motive here, he doesn't necessarily have his own plan, but he is trying to figure out everyone else's in order to choose which one he'll elect himself to be a part of. The other Mark, not to be confused with me, Ben, Samuel, Steve and Yung-Lee are the hardest to predict because they rarely talk to anyone other than themselves, and they all keep themselves in a different room to where most other people are located at one time, apart from when eating or showering.

And then there's Harry. He's been following my messages, therefore he doesn't have his own plan, and as far as I'm aware, he hasn't told anyone which tells me that he is the right candidate to join me. He minds his own business and occasionally stands up for what he thinks is right. I don't trust him, just the same as I don't trust anyone, but I guess you could say I like him.

I have waited a few minutes so it doesn't look as if I'm following him to the toilet room. Also Bill is sitting opposite to me and he may have thought my pen falling from my pocket was a signal for Harry, talking in silence, in code. I have to be careful because there is a spy here, we are all aware of that, or potentially more than one, and in my view it could be one of fourteen, excluding myself and Harry. I turn over my shoulder discreetly and see that Mohammed is now undressing and entering the shower room, it's the perfect opportunity.

I stand up and pretend to walk in a little circle, slowly around the centre bench as if I'm bored and have no thoughts processing, just as Bill or anyone who may enter the room would expect to see, and suddenly I trail off, through the left-hand open doorway past the shower room and into the toilet room.

It's empty, apart from the feet underneath the second cubicle, which is the middle one, and I enter the third one, farthest from the door, then lock myself inside and perch on the edge of the toilet seat.

Silence, apart from the occasional drip of a loose tap.

I write: *Book*, upside-down on the palm of my right hand so when I slide it under the panel, which separates the two cubicles, he will be able to read it.

Harry places the book in my hand and I transport it into my cubicle. I turn to a random page in the middle and write in bold letters: *Do not talk. Just write. Thank you for coming. I have a plan. Do you wish to join?*

I place the pen in the middle, between the pages, and close it before passing it under the panel and into the enormous hands of Harry.

I don't bother with telling him that he can trust me because, as far as he knows, he can't. It would have been a lie, those words are never said anymore. Instead, he will have to listen to what his stomach tells him and calculate his chances. I know he isn't a spy because…well, I don't know, I just assume, and assuming in this day and age is extremely dangerous, but I'm too afraid to leave by myself and enter the dark unknown, to re-enter a world none of us fully understand anymore.

His hand appears under the panel, holding the book out to me. I retrieve it and open it to the page with the pen and it reads: *Thank you for the invite. This could be a setup, but I guess there's no point in asking, so we'll just have to work together. What plan?*

I reply: *You're welcome. I guess we will. An escape plan, in two days. I am offering you a chance to leave here. You're the only person I would ask. Keep quiet about it, do not talk to me or about me or be anywhere near me. Stay clear of Mohammed, he is watching you.*

We trade messages for the next couple of minutes, not speaking the entire time in case anyone enters or is secretly listening, or if there are microphones, but I am against that theory. I don't believe there are cameras either, otherwise the murders and suicides, and the escape before would have been intervened by the guards.

I tell him, in writing, that he will receive a sign and will know when I want to arrange our next meeting tomorrow. I then tell him to take the book and pretend to the others he is still reading it, but make sure not to turn to a page that has been written on, and to keep it safe and out of anyone's reach, and finally I tell him to leave the toilet room and return to whatever he was doing as normal.

After he has exited the toilet room I try to unscrew the pen to shake the ink cartridge because the last couple of messages had to be forced to write as the ink is running low.

I had stolen the pen about two months ago when the paper was being passed around for people to put their names down for garden duty, and have kept it with me ever since, only using it in the last month to contact Harry to join in on the plan I have been constructing for three months.

I've made a fatal mistake. The cartridge leaks and two large drops of black ink rain down onto the bottom of my t-shirt, forming two large blotches that spread out to eventually meet each other in a stream and form one large evident black stain on the white material.

"Shit," I whisper, another mistake. I haven't spoken, not even to myself, for so long the word hurts my throat and feels foreign.

It's not like I can hide the t-shirt, it's all I have for the next two days until I'm gone and it isn't like I can replace it with someone else's during the night to set them up and save myself because we all have our own separate numbers on the backs of them.

I leave the cubicle and wash the pen in one of the two sinks, then tighten it and slip it into my pocket, before washing the word I had written on one of my scarred hands and the ink that has smudged over my fingers, and then I attempt to dampen the stain on my t-shirt but it isn't making any difference. I have no choice but to tuck it into my trousers to hide it and hope that no one will notice the difference. Of course they will, I never tuck my t-shirt in, they will know something has changed and therefore my mind isn't static, but it is all I can do.

"Two days, I'll be gone in two days," I whisper into the mirror, smiling, feeling pleasure now in hearing my own voice. There aren't any cameras behind the mirror, I am positive, everyone else is just paranoid.

Two days, that's all it is, I tell myself whilst leaving the toilet room. I pass the shower room, getting a glance from Mohammed whom I'm sure would have given the same to Harry, who is now sat on the centre bench 'reading' as I walk by, and then I enter the bedroom, pass Elliott sat on his bed second from the door on the right, pass Nick on the fourth bed from the far end on the left, and take my place at the very far end bed on the left to lie down.

Chapter 12

Someone has just entered the bedroom. I don't have to pay attention or even look up to know it's Marcus, even without having to look at the cuts on his palms, it's the way his presence is so quiet and his movements are so timid, as he strolls through the pathway between the beds to take his place at the end.

The only other person in the room, other than us two, is Nick who has been lying down for the last ten minutes with his pillows propped up against the wall and his back resting on them and his duvet over himself with his knees up underneath, almost creating a tent-affect, and his hands are doing something underneath. Some would say masturbating, others might think he is just itching, but I know better, he's obviously hiding something, but it doesn't bother me, I'm not watching him, I'm lying here thinking about the letter from Jane that now stores itself underneath my foot in my left shoe, but more so at this moment I'm thinking about George.

I'm anxious, waiting for his return, wondering if he's done the unspeakable but the very possible deed of running out on me and having escaped by himself after digging the last half a foot of soil from our hole. If he gets there before I do, then my arrangement with Jane will be sabotaged and we'll both remain trapped here, separated, maybe until we both die alone.

Unexpectedly, as I'm having that thought, George appears at the doorway. He has returned from garden duty and he comes round the corner to his bed which is the closest to the doorway on my side of the room, next to me on my left.

I am surprised to see him, I was having thoughts that the guards were going to enter and inform us that he has disappeared. The relief I feel must be evident as I spin my legs round and place my feet down on the floor, sitting up to face him as he sits down opposite me.

He pauses before speaking, hesitating, whilst checking over my shoulder that Nick and Marcus aren't looking, and speaks in a very low tone with a serious excitement in his eyes he is trying so hard to prevent from being clear, "It's ready."

I don't turn over my shoulder, I don't want anyone present thinking that we're discussing something we want to remain private between the two of us, but I glance sideways out of the doorway to make sure no one is entering or sitting on the closest bench in the main room.

"Really?" I ask, as if I don't believe it, but of course I know the hole is dug, it wouldn't have taken him long.

"Our names are on the waiting list for two days' time, so as long as we're both chosen for garden duty, in less than forty-eight hours we will be gone from here."

"What if only one of our names is on the duty list?" I'm not sure why I said that, I don't want him suspecting me of leaving him behind because it's now obvious that he wouldn't do the same to me, he has returned for me which makes me feel tremendously guilty.

"Then I guess we'll just have to wait a little longer until both of our names are chosen," he replies with a sense of suspicion and maybe a little worry.

I nod and say nothing, feeling the two letters from Jane, one from today and the other from a month ago, both securely hidden in either of my shoes.

"Who was the letter from?" asks George. He is now glaring at me, almost examining my clothes and my bed, wondering to himself where I have put it, unaware that there are actually two letters.

I stare back, wetting my lips and trying to process an answer that is plausible and will also divert him from asking me. If he knows it's from Jane, although he doesn't know of her existence, then he will fear about my contribution to our escaping together. If he knows it's something as important to me as it is, then he will want to read it. Remember, none of us are friends here. I may like George but I don't trust him.

"I haven't opened it yet," I say, itching my elbows nervously. George nods, looks around the room, wondering if I'm lying, unsure as to whom he has chosen to plan an escape with and if his chances are at risk because of a letter, and then he returns to my attention.

"We'll have to be careful not to discuss anything to do with the hole from now until we leave, hopefully in two days," he says, going back to the original topic where I feel more comfortable. I can see he keeps looking over in the direction of Nick, probably wondering what his hands are doing under his duvet.

Chapter 13

Everyone here has secrets, I think to myself, sitting upright in my bed with my back against the pillows, the duvet over my bent knees, my eyes trading exchanges over in the corner of the room to where Elliott and George are talking. They're talking about me, or at least wondering what I'm doing, but they're also planning something, they have secrets. Secrets from the rest of us, secrets from each other, just like I have secrets, we all do.

Everyone here is plotting and scheming. Everyone has plans. Everyone has intentions. You can read people and see they're working things out, you can feel their movements all around you, you can hear them thinking. You know when someone has changed, possibly gained new knowledge or information on something, or if they're attitude towards this way of life and their destiny has altered, you know by just looking at them.

My name may be Nick but most of them here would probably refer to me as something else. I'm not very much liked here, I wasn't liked much in my past life before the war. I didn't have anyone before and I don't have anyone now, but I don't need anyone, I don't want anyone, all I need and want is myself. I am all that matters to me. Do you think that's the wrong way to be? Fuck you.

I want to get out of here, like the rest of them, but being unpopular makes it difficult, even I know that it's impossible to escape from here without the help of another survivor. I am waiting for a plan to come about, someone else's thoughts to slip from their mind, for one of them to make a mistake, and then I will act and be part of their plan without them even agreeing. If I know their plan, then they will have no choice but to involve me, or else I could fuck up their chances of leaving.

I've decided to focus on the weakest character. Most of them would say Marcus, the young, silent kid that lays two beds away from me, is the weakest, but what am I going to get out of him? He doesn't communicate and he has cuts on his hands so I'm pretty sure he's self-harming, which isn't any use to me. So the weakest link to me is John. He won't fight back or argue, he will do what I say, and I have told him, warned him, that if he knows of any escape plans that are being discussed or going to take place then he has to inform me or otherwise I will cut his balls off.

I dream of getting out of here, finding some place that managed to stay standing after 'The Bomb', and hold up there for a while, maybe find myself some bitch that has survived to fuck endlessly. I used to fuck whores even when the law of 2055 banned sexual intercourse, and now there is no law, there is no police, at least not in the same way as there used to be, and I intend to do what the fuck I want when I get my freedom.

Underneath my pillow is the bread roll I took from John earlier, I'll eat that under my duvet tonight, hours after the second meal, so I'll go to sleep with a full stomach, more full than anyone else's. None of them will know this, apart from John, and I smile knowing that fact.

I peer under the duvet to make sure I haven't messed up what I've been doing for probably twenty minutes now, and to be cautious that I haven't cut my fingers off.

I concentrate on the shard of metal I ripped from the bottom of the first cubicle in the toilet room only yesterday, just a three inch sheet of metal that tore off the corner of the door like frozen foil, having had no screw attached and more or less hanging off. I just helped myself. I am bending it into a shape so the end I am holding is thicker and wider so it fits into the palm of my hand, and the other end of it is like a razor which I am carving by using a smaller piece which I tore off. I am making my own tool, my very own weapon. If the guards find it, which they won't unless I show it to them or someone tells them, then they will confiscate it, so I have been keeping it under my mattress, just like everyone hides things under their mattresses here. As long as it doesn't go missing, it is well known here that people go rooting around your things if they have reason to believe you are hiding something worthy. The last thing I want is me being defenceless, knowing someone here has my weapon on them but not knowing who, and wondering if they intend to use it on *me*.

I intend to use it when necessary, whether that be on John to threaten him more or to get information from someone else, or to demand a ticket to someone else's escape route or on a guard as a last solution if it means getting out of here.

I'm just buying time, carving away at my knife and watching the others to see who might be the first unfortunate one on the end of it.

Day 742

Chapter 1

On the morning of the seven hundred and forty-second day inside The Vault, it was made clear that sixteen had become fifteen. Someone was no longer present. Someone had disappeared during the night.

Samuel had vanished. No sign. Nothing. No one knew anything. No one saw anything. Or so they said.

The letter he had received yesterday from his 'sister' was suspected to have been from someone who had potentially played part in his escape. That made everyone else suspect Elliott, wondering whom his letter was from and where he was keeping it hidden.

Although Elliott and Harry both had plans taking place, separate plans, they both made the right decision to continue their usual routine, in order to avoid any suspicion from anyone, by doing their workout: pulling up on the metal bar in the left-hand doorway of the shower room, doing press-ups on the floor and using the benches in the main room to stretch.

Neither of them said a word to each other during their fitness regime.

With each muscle being worked, with each drop of sweat seeping from a pore, with every vein pulsing under the surface of the skin, the two of them were deep in thought. Harry was thinking about Marcus and the escape plan he was waiting to be a part of: leaving tomorrow. Elliott was thinking about Jane, the letter, the hole, George: leaving tomorrow.

George was sitting on a bench watching Elliott work out, Mohammed was standing by the window watching both Elliott and Harry work out, Bill was sitting on the bench near the bedroom doorway stroking his rat's head inside his jacket pocket, Marcus was lying on his bed, facing the wall and examining a new scar on his palm, Nick was lying on his bed feeling the jagged edge of his homemade knife inside his trouser pocket, Steve was pacing up and down the bedroom with an expression of panic, Kris was playing cards in the playroom with Hal and Roger, Mark was in the second cubicle of the toilet room not feeling very well, and John and Ben were taking showers.

All deep in thought, not a single one of them was speaking.

The red light above The Door died and the green light came alive. The bolts were being unlocked, the handle was turning with a creak of rusty metal and then the guards entered.

Everyone gathered in the main room, some sitting, some standing.

It was clear that the guards already knew something. Today there were four of them: Anthony, Lucas and two others. They knew that someone wasn't present. They knew before they had entered. Before they even allowed anyone to rush forward for their first meal of the day, the guards informed them that Samuel had gone missing and managed to escape during the night. His whereabouts were unknown. They asked if anyone knew anything.

Everyone was on edge, all eyes probed the room, sizing each other and wondering who might be harbouring any knowledge, or may have even been an accomplice.

Not a single person said a single word. Not a single person took a single step forward.

The two unfamiliar guards grabbed Steve without question and dragged him away, kicking and screaming, before Anthony and Lucas remained, allowing everyone to help themselves to their food which today was two slices of stale toast each, without butter, and of course the flasks were a quarter filled with tea.

Everyone ate in further silence, avoiding eye contact with each other.

The guards waited until everyone had finished their meal, unaware that Nick had once again decided to take John's toast and slip it into his pocket, before they collected the paper plates, wheeled the trolley away, glanced around the main room once more, left the survivors to themselves and locked The Door.

The green light went out and the red light came back on.

New theories in all their heads were arising. The guards knew about the escape before they had entered and they had taken Steve away without any proof of him being involved or knowing something, so either there *were* cameras within The Vault or there *was* a spy. If there were cameras, then surely the guards would have been able to intervene with the escape? So surely there must be a spy? Or several spies? But the spy(s) must have had a way of communicating with the guards and sending them information. That was a fact. How did they transfer the information through the walls and through The Door of The Vault? Did someone have a secret passageway? Did someone have a key to leave during the night to arrange secret meetings with the guards? Was this person, or these people, handing others over to receive benefits of some sort or protection for themselves? These were all questions everyone attempted to answer by themselves. No one spoke but everyone thought the same.

But the big question on everyone's minds during that meal was: *Who* is the spy?

Chapter 2

"May God punish you for your sins!" I cry, once the guards have left, pointing my finger at Nick who sits on the edge of the bench closest to the bedroom doorway as I stand by The Door with the red light burning above.

I've had enough of being bullied, threatened and treated the way I am by him. I can't take it anymore. I haven't eaten two meals of my own in three days because he takes them from me.

"You what?" he replies, as if innocently, but bitterly, not believing I can talk to him in such a way. He believes I am his property, he owns me and can do what he wants with me.

"I want my food back!" I scream. Now those who had gone to the shower room are reappearing round the corner, and those from the playroom as well, and those from the bedroom, along with Bill sitting next to Nick, Mohammed standing at the windows and Harry sitting on the centre bench reading, they are all now looking at me, stunned by my shouting, wondering what Nick has done to me.

"What food?" he replies, almost cackling.

"It's these types of actions that separate us as humans! It's this world that has ceased to exist, not the human race, we are survivors underneath God's thumb. He allows us the will to continue. How dare you attempt to deny me my right to survive? How dare you attempt to deny me my right to the only luxuries I am given? God gives me bread, you take it from my hands. God gives me water, and you take it from my hands!" I am now screaming at the top of my lungs, my face is burning bright red, my eyes are watering and my breath is causing my glasses to steam over slightly.

"Shut the fuck up!" barks Nick. "Stop preaching! Nobody gives a fuck what you have to say! God isn't going to save us! He has failed us!"

"We have failed! God is disappointed with his children! And those that cannot seek repent are those that will not receive mercy! You are an example of why we will never change our ways!"

"John, what's wrong?" asks a voice from the back of the room, I'm not sure who it's coming from.

"Give him his food back, Nick!" someone else shouts.

"I haven't got his fucking food!" he yells aggressively.

"Man has stripped me of everything in life! Now you want to take more from me!" I exclaim, saliva spraying from my tongue, tears forming in my eyes.

"You want to fucking watch yourself!" Nick warns, pointing at me, shuffling his feet. He's boiling over. Suddenly, the room has become too hot; I picture myself fleeing outside to cool down or even living by myself in Antarctica where I can survive on God's land.

"No! It is you that should watch yourself!" I reply.

"Yeah?" he asks, standing, striding across the room towards me with a violent essence around him.

"Nick, just give him his food and everyone will be happy!" someone else shouts, I think it's George.

As Nick reaches me he hits me backwards into The Door, knocking me to the ground, causing me to crawl on the floor to retrieve my glasses as blood trickles down my nose.

This is the most excitement everyone has experienced in a long time, so they all just sit and stand, watching, not reacting. Apart from one…

A book falls to the floor.

Harry has risen to his feet.

Nick goes flying across the room and lands hard on his back, he grunts slightly before glancing up to face giant Harry who now towers over him with a fierce guise and clenched fists. He had grabbed Nick by the throat before launching him away from me like a missile.

"You fucking leave him alone! Or next time you'll have me to fight instead, go it?" exclaims Harry. Nick may have boiled but Harry was on a different level; for a brief moment I picture the nuclear explosions.

There is silence in the room.

Harry bends over and picks up the toast, *my* toast, that had fallen from Nick's pockets as he landed on the ground, and he hands it over to me before snatching up his book which had landed open on the floor. It was as if something had been inside the book that he hadn't wanted anyone to see, because his eyes had lit up when he realised he had dropped it, and then he suddenly turned a couple of pages before sitting down on the bench again to continue reading.

Nick gets to his feet and storms away to the bedroom, sulking and trying to regain the dominant and intimidating presence in his walk.

"Thank you," I say, getting up from the floor, wiping my nose with the back of my hand and holding the toast in my other, whilst everyone else returns to whatever they had been doing a minute ago.

"Don't thank me, otherwise you'll be rewarding my aggressive and violent reaction which would make you a hypocrite," Harry replies, not looking up to me.

"I wasn't thanking you for protecting me." His eyebrows collapse inwards in confusion. "I was thanking you for not seeing me as a number, but rather a human."

Harry turns his head, stares at me for a while without saying anything and then nods in acceptance.

I head to the toilet room to clean my nose and to eat my toast by myself in a cubicle.

Chapter 3

Twenty minutes pass by after the fight between Nick and John, which I felt the need to resolve because no one else was going to do anything. I keep my eye on Mohammed, making sure he isn't in the same room as me before I act. I wait for him to go to the shower room before I stand from my bench and head to the bedroom, Marcus having entered ten minutes before me.

I pass Elliott lying on his bed with his duvet over him, I can't tell if he's asleep or crying or what. I then pass Nick sitting on his bed, his duvet also over him, there's movement underneath it, and he gives me an angry stare. Everyone is up to something today.

I come to Steve's bed which is two beds away from Marcus's at the end. Steve's bed will be removed soon. We all know he won't be returning. So will Samuel's bed. He won't be returning either. Two less beds, two less people, in one day. Fourteen remaining.

I then pass Hal's bed next to Marcus's. Marcus is sitting on his bed, he has been waiting for me.

This is our next meeting. He had given me a sign during our meal by looking in my direction and closing his eyes for several seconds, pausing, then opening them where they landed on me again, as if it were one very long blink. Luckily Mohammed had been busy eating his meal and hadn't been looking in either of our directions.

"You should give this a read," I say clearly, making sure everyone will hear so they'll be aware that I am only handing Marcus my book.

He nods, being careful not to speak, as Elliott and Nick both look over.

I head over to my bed and lie down, not looking in his direction, just keeping to myself.

Marcus gets underneath his duvet, rolls himself over to face the wall as if he is reading in bed, when in actual fact I know he will be removing his pen from his pocket and will be writing a message in the book for me. I noticed he had had his t-shirt tucked into his trousers, which was out of the ordinary, he must have a reason for it I guess.

Minutes later he climbs out of bed, walks over to me and hands me the book back without speaking.

"Not your type, no?" I ask, again loud and clear so the others will hear. Marcus goes back to his bed, gets under the duvet and pretends to sleep. "He probably can't read," I say, allowing the others to believe that I think the same of Marcus as they all do.

I open the book, flick through several pages to find a new message, and finally I find it written across the middle of a page, the ink is a little smudged and the words have streaks running from the ends. *His ink is either running low or the pen is broken*, I think to myself. Maybe that's why he has tucked his t-shirt in, because he has a stain on it? As long as the ink lasts until we no longer need to send messages and we're out of here then it'll be fine. The message reads*: **Tonight. When the final person gets into bed. Count to a thousand. Check Bill to your right, Roger to your left and Hal opposite you. You are fortunately surrounded by the eldest so hopefully they will be fast asleep, but be wary: they may be old but nobody here is deaf.**

Crawl out of bed, crawl across the floor as silently as possible. When you reach my bed you will find me and the escape. See you on the other side. Good luck. Do not inform anyone of this information, I know you're smart enough not to.

On the opposite page he has sketched an outline of The Vault and marked an **X** on his bed to make clear where I need to go, as if I need reminding, but I guess he is taking precaution in case of last minute anxiety.

What escape could there be at his bed? It has to be underneath, I think to myself. And still I ask: Why has he chosen me?

I reread the message over and over before tucking the book under my mattress and lying back, closing my eyes, and going over and over the plan in my mind so I will have it clearly mapped out before the big move tonight.

Chapter 4

I'm holding the letter from Jane under my duvet, the second letter. Fortunately, George is in the shower room so I have some time to myself to plan out my plot.

He has been removed from the equation, I have already decided that. The escape I am participating in is for myself and Jane, that's all I really care about. Do I feel guilty? Only slightly, because I do like George, but not enough to leave Jane behind.

George could join us? I think to myself. It wouldn't make any difference, as long as we're both on the list for garden duty then all we have to do is meet Jane as I have arranged and the three of us could crawl under the hole together. It would probably make the escape easier because then I don't have to worry about removing George from the plan. But then…would he hold Jane and me back? If I tell him that there is going to be a third person joining us, will he become paranoid and fear that something is going to go wrong because it means changing the plan slightly? Or…worst case scenario, what if his name is on the list and mine isn't, and he decides to leave without me anyway, not only trapping me but also Jane? If he escapes, then the guards will discover the hole and I'll be back to square one, only by myself.

No, I shake my head. Jane is my priority, she is my plan. George has been removed from the equation, it's final.

Tapping the letter against my left hand and rubbing my index finger down the glue of the envelope, I'm staring into open space at the wall opposite me, just above Mark's bed on the other side of the room, his is to the right of Samuel's which will be removed soon, but I'm not thinking about that, I'm now trying to work out two very important things.

The first one is that I need to remove George's name from the garden duty list for tomorrow and make sure that I get chosen. But how?

The second one is that I need to send Jane a letter, which she will receive today, to let her know I will definitely meet her, without George or anyone knowing. But how?

It's these two thoughts I'm holding when all of a sudden shouting, hollering, panicking, and crying for help comes spilling across the main room like a howling echo and into the bedroom. I quickly scan round the room and notice that Harry, Nick and Marcus are all sitting up and looking in the direction of the doorway, wondering what is happening out there.

Slyly, underneath my duvet, I slip the envelope back inside my shoe underneath my foot again.

As I get to the doorway and lean against the wooden frame, I'm stunned to see John and Ben dragging Mark through the left-hand doorway of the shower room and out into the main room. It's clear that Mark isn't conscious. His eyelids are tightly shut. There is dark blood running down his chin, leaving a trail behind him, and speckles are sprayed all over his shirt and trousers as if by a careless painter.

They lay him down on the ground and turn him on his side, the blood pours from his mouth and forms a puddle on the floor. John runs to The Door and bangs repeatedly, screaming, "We need help!"

By now the others in the bedroom are standing behind me and looking out, those in the shower room are standing in the doorways and looking out and those in the playroom are also doing the same.

Did he slip in the toilet room and smash his face on a sink? Did he attempt suicide? Was he attacked?

The red light goes out and the green light comes on.

The guards, Anthony and Lucas, enter with their weapons ready, preparing to have to settle an issue between us. But they take less than five seconds to realise there isn't a fight.

"What happened?" bellows Anthony as he approaches Mark's still body, with Lucas standing by The Door.

"He's not breathing! He was in a cubicle coughing up blood, he's been in there all morning!" replies John. "God bless him," he whispers not so quietly.

Anthony kneels down, places two fingers against Mark's neck to find his pulse and then looks back up to all of us, looking from doorway to doorway.

"He's dead," he says sharply.

Anthony puts his machine gun around his back with the strap securing it in place, then grabs Mark's wrists and drags him out of The Door and into the hallway.

"You two found him so you two shall clean that up," orders Lucas, pointing at the blood and gazing at John and Ben, before he closes The Door and locks it, and the two lights alter again.

Another person gone, another bed will be removed. Three in one day. Thirteen remaining.

What a day this is becoming, I'm thinking, finding it hard to take my eyes away from the blood which John and Ben start discussing about how to clean up.

For a brief second I feel as if I'm being watched so I look up further away and see George standing in the left-hand doorway to the shower room, he's standing there with a towel round his waist and he's looking back at me with Mohammed approaching behind him. He's watching me, trying to work out what I'm thinking about.

Chapter 5

I'm watching Elliott very carefully. He suddenly feels uncomfortable and heads to the playroom where Kris, Roger and Hal re-enter.

"He'll be at the window," says Mohammed who has appeared by my side in his towel.

"What?" I ask, turning to him.

"Elliott. You're wondering where he is going and what he's thinking about. It's okay to admit, I know you two talk a lot and you're obviously planning something together, everyone here knows that," he smiles.

"What about a window?" I ask curiously.

"He spends a lot of time every day at the back window in the playroom, usually when you're in the shower or if you're having a nap because he knows you'll ask questions. He usually does it when no one is in the playroom, maybe just after the first meal of the day, and he tries to eat as quickly as possible so he can be the first to finish and the first in there," Mohammed discloses, flicking a finger over to the playroom.

"Why? There's nothing wrong with looking out a window. Elliott just dreams a lot, he pictures himself…"

"I know, I know," Mohammed nods, smirking, almost cutting me off to correct me. "I know what you're going to say. We all look out the windows and imagine running away from here, we all plan that anyhow, and it's no secret. But Elliott isn't looking out the window, that particular window, because he's lost in his imagination. Elliott has a reason to be staring out that very window each day. He's been doing it the last month or so, I've been keeping an eye on him."

"You keep an eye on everyone." Mohammed laughs and nods as if agreeing.

"I've found that you can learn a lot about your surroundings if you keep an eye on them," he says gently, attempting to teach me something.

"So why does he stare out the window?"

"Who knows? But in my judgement, I believe he knows someone that lives in the vault opposite."

"You mean one of the women?"

"Yes," he nods, losing his smile, now replacing it with seriousness.

"Who?"

"I don't know," he shrugs. "Maybe that's what you should find out. Oh, but you should know…" he starts to say, as I turn my back to re-enter the showers, "the letter he received yesterday wasn't the first one. He had another about four weeks ago, you weren't here. I bet he never told you about that, did he?"

I feel myself sinking inside, I feel the plan that I have been working on with Elliott for the last four months is sinking too. The soil is being poured back in, the hole is closing up and the locks on The Door will never be removed again. An overwhelming sensation of isolation, even more than we have had to endure for the last two years, is suddenly swallowing me.

As I remove my towel to take my shower, which had initially been disturbed by the discovery of Mark's dead body, I think about Elliott and tell myself I need to find out what he's hiding from me before we leave together tomorrow. *If* we leave together tomorrow.

I see Mohammed removing his towel as he dries himself and begins to get dressed. I'm wondering if what he has told me is a lie. I'm hoping it is. He has fed me the information and no longer gives me attention. Once he is dressed he leaves through the doorway like a man with an intention. There are plenty of them here.

Chapter 6

Today is exciting, I think to myself, as I avoid stepping in the blood on the floor of the main room that had come from Mark's stomach and out of his mouth, whilst John and Ben move around gently, attempting to wipe it up with Mark's old sponge which will no longer be needed.

Samuel escaped and no one seems to know how, apart from Steve who was taken away by the guards, and Mark died from health-related issues. There was the fight between Nick and John which Harry resolved. Elliott is spending less and less time around George and is staying farther and farther away from him. I also happen to have stored myself other information about certain individuals, information which I have only recently conquered to discover, information I believe no one else is aware of, which makes me feel superior and makes today even more exciting, and because I feel like sharing some of that information with certain people it makes me smile.

Mohammed the Master, they should call me.

I laugh to myself as I cross the main room, fiddling with my lucky coin in my pocket, and arrive at the doorway of the bedroom.

For some reason everyone seems to have their duvets over them today, and not because they're cold, but because they have something to hide.

Nick, I couldn't care what he's up to, he's never getting out of here. It's Harry I am interested in. It's Harry I approach. I sit down on Roger's bed and Harry looks over to me.

"Yes?" he asks.

"I know," I reply, whispering, smirking.

"What?"

"Don't worry, I'm not going to say anything to anyone, I just want you to be aware that I know. I think it's important that you're aware."

"Aware of what? What the fuck are you talking about?" asks Harry, sitting upright in his bed, trying not to speak too loudly but finding it hard to prevent the obvious anger in his voice from rising, and attempting to look perplexed when in actual fact it's completely evident he knows exactly what I am talking about. He's frightened. Everyone is frightened in this new world, but he is now really shitting himself.

"Harry, drop the act." There's a pause between us, he's waiting for my next word and I'm waiting for him to interrupt me with more fake innocence. "You accused me of being the messenger and I haven't yet received an apology." Another pause.

"I'm sorry," Harry says timidly and hesitantly, oblivious to the fact that he has just given something away.

"By you apologising, that tells me that you know I'm not the messenger so therefore you know who is."

"You're very clever," Harry begins to say, "but do you really think you should be threatening me?"

"Why?" I ask, grinning, leaning forward. "What do you possibly have to threaten me with? Strength?" I snort. "We both know that can't get you out of here."

Harry shuffles in his bed and straightens up even more, as if this is the first time since I have sat down that he has truly started to listen and become interested. We both quickly gaze around the room and make sure that no one else is looking. It's only Nick that we have caught the attention of, who is busy doing something underneath his duvet, I believe he is making a weapon to attack someone or a tool to use to escape, and there's Marcus who is asleep but I believe is actually pretending to be.

"I know Marcus is the messenger," I whisper. "I know because I saw the ink stain on his t-shirt which all of a sudden he has decided to tuck into his trousers. I know he is the one who owns the pen therefore he is the one that has been writing to you in the books. I know the two of you have been avoiding me and that you have been arranging meetings in secret. He's not stupid like everyone believes, and he can talk, can't he?"

Harry nods in defeat.

There's silence for a few seconds between us. Harry has nothing to say. I examine the room again, Bill has entered and is walking down the pathway towards his bed which is at the far end on the right-hand side, the bed on the other side of Harry's.

"I'm not here to threaten you," I say, returning my focus on Harry who has begun to sweat and turn red in the face.

"Then what do you want?"

"I just wanted to let you know that I know, that's all. To keep my options open."

Bill may be old and he may spend most of his time sitting down, but he can walk when he wants to. Suddenly, he is at my side, he passes us and sits down on his bed. I look up at him and smile for longer than usual, without saying anything. Bill looks concerned, almost worried. I'm telling him, from thought and expression, that I know something about him, and it's the truth, I do know something about Bill which no one else seems to be aware of, but I'll save that for later.

Bill looks away, almost feeling intimidated, and then rolls over on his bed to face the wall. Harry has noticed my gaze towards Bill and looks to me to almost question.

"Be careful," I whisper to him, pointing towards Bill, before I walk away.

I take a seat on one of the benches in the main room. The blood has now been cleaned up from the floor. No one else is in here but John who is sitting on the centre bench, exhausted and looking pale.

I know how Samuel escaped. I can't tell anyone for two reasons: 1) they will suspect I knew about it and was involved in assisting him, I will be reported to the guards by the spy, and just so you know: there definitely is a spy, and the guards will take me away like they did with Steve, and 2) others will attempt to use the same escape route, ruining my chances of using it, and if the spy discovers this then once again it will be reported to the guards and they will block it up.

I didn't know of Samuel's escape until this morning just like everyone else, apart from Steve of course, may he rest in peace, God knows what the guards will do to him. I happened to work it out by myself this morning as I entered the playroom, I'm surprised no one else knows about it, it's obvious when you stand in the middle of the room. The guards don't know either, unless

Steve has spilled the beans and told them, and the spy can't have told them because Samuel had escaped, therefore, meaning the spy hadn't known about it until today.

I will be using it is as my Plan A. Involving myself in Marcus's and Harry's escape is my Plan B.

Unless Steve tells the guards or anyone else secretly knows or if anyone figures it out within the next twenty-four hours, I am going to stay completely quiet and avoid entering the playroom to deter any attention to it. That escape route is my ticket out of here.

Chapter 7

"Whose turn is it?" asks George, looking over the chessboard we have set up, on the table in the playroom, which we had taken down from the top of one of the bookcases. No one else is in the room. Kris, Hal and Roger had finished their game of cards several minutes ago before George had entered to find me staring out of the window where Jane stared back. I'm not sure if he had seen her or not though and it's making me feel uneasy.

Neither of us are paying attention to the game, we have only made about four or five moves, and it is clear from the lack of conversation that both of us have things on our minds.

"I don't know," I say, "mine…no, yours, I think," sighing without care.

George doesn't move, he doesn't pick up a chess piece or even look at the board to decide on what he is going to do next. He isn't thinking about the game, he is thinking about me.

"Who's the letter from?" he asks bluntly, leaning back in his hair with interest.

This isn't two friends playing chess, this isn't a trivia, this isn't a test or an interview, this is an interrogation. He has been wanting to ask me that question since I received it yesterday, he had asked me already and I had told him I hadn't opened it, but I decide there's no point in hiding it anymore. I have a feeling he knows I have opened it anyway and I had seen him earlier when he had been standing in the shower room doorway after the incident with Mark dying, he had been watching me, and Mohammed had been standing near him which was not a good sign.

I exhale slowly and blink gently, preparing myself to reveal to him a secret or two, hopefully neither of which will destroy the plan I have which will advertently be against him.

"When we first came here two years ago you asked me about who I lost in the war and I told you my whole family died, and that was the truth."

"Yeah, I remember," he says, nodding with sympathy and eyes that attempt to pry a little deeper.

"And you asked me how I survived if they all died. You asked me where I had been."

"Yeah," he nods, his voice soft.

"Well I wasn't there when they died. I wasn't at home." I look away and stare at the ground as I begin to have flashbacks of that day, the words coming from my mouth reliving the moment. "I was visiting a friend. A female friend." My eyes peer up to George who is leaning on the table with his elbows, his face contorted, as he lights a cigarette with a match and blows smoke in my face. "I had been having an affair. Her name is Jane and I love her and…" I pause, waiting to tell him the climax of the tale, "and she's alive."

George doesn't say anything and I hadn't expected him to.

"There isn't a day that goes by since then that I haven't felt guilt for not being with my family, for not comforting my wife and children when The Bomb happened, but when it did happen I was thankful to be alive, I can admit that much. Jane and I spent the next two years living together, surviving, loving, in her place in the country, until the military came and brought us here. Obviously I knew she had survived the war but when we were captured we were separated before being brought here. When I arrived, I searched the list but never found her name and ever since I have believed maybe she had died on the journey or something terrible had happened to her with the soldiers, or maybe she had managed to escape them and flee back into the country. If I had bothered to check the list again though, I would have realised her name was on there, I guess it could have been added later on because she arrived after me, I don't know, it doesn't matter, because about a month ago I received a letter. It was from Jane. She sent me another one yesterday, the one you're asking about."

I can see the panic and overwhelmingly terrified expression on George's innocent face begin to swarm his skin in paramount effect, and the heartache in his blue, teary eyes shows a man that is dishevelled. It's possible that he is sad for me, but I am convinced he is worried for his own chances.

"So…what are you doing to do?" he asks in a croaky voice, each word broken.

"Well, I'm going to stick to the original plan that you and I made. We're leaving here tomorrow," I whisper.

He doesn't say anything. He doesn't believe me.

"I can't risk my own chances of escaping," I say. "She's no longer in my life, I've gotten used to being without her," I lie.

"So you're just going to leave her behind?" he asks, probably wondering that if I can do that to the woman I love then I can do the same to him, someone who, outside of here, means nothing to me.

"Yes. I can't save her. This is the only chance that you and I may ever get."

"So we're going through with this, you're sure of that?" he asks, the first time he has asked since four months ago when we had started digging the hole.

"Yeah, I promise. This time tomorrow we'll be gone."

"The war changed everyone," George sighs, hinting something.

"Don't get me wrong," I say, leaning on the table, edging closer to him, "I remember when I was a child and I saw a picture of a tiger. I thought it was the most beautiful, majestic thing I had ever seen, and now they're a thing of the past, pre-historic. If you take away all the beauty from the world, what are we left with? There is nothing here for me or you or anyone! Jane isn't part of my life anymore, it wouldn't be the same! The world has changed and so have we!

"And of course I dream of making love, just like every one of us sex-deprived humans does! But even that would have changed. It's no longer a necessity. Since the law of 2055 I've gotten used to being without it," I lie again. "I don't need Jane in my life."

I sit back as does he, both staring at the chessboard but not making a move.

"Why do you think they haven't allowed us to mingle with the women?" he asks, changing the topic, puffing more smoke and caressing the head of the white queen on the board.

"What?"

"Well, the law in 2055 was introduced to prevent reproduction because we were overpopulated, but now there are hardly any humans alive and people are still dropping dead from the effects of the war and might still be for a long time, so surely they should be worried about the population being too low and us humans becoming extinct?"

"I don't know," I say, shrugging my shoulders. "We'll probably never know. Nuclear warfare is the worst discovery ever made by man. A creation of destruction. It's the ultimate irony, just like the abortion."

"I believe they wanted a war. The law of 2055 could have taken generations to reduce the population, so it wasn't a case of culling or controlling the numbers, they just needed to act fast, and they needed a war to change the world."

"It wasn't a war," I reply, losing my nerve not wanting to talk about it.

"The war of 2057? The Bomb? The apocalyptic, doomsday, World War Three, end of the world, fucking…war of all wars, which has killed billions and nearly ended the world…?"

"Yes," I say. "It wasn't a war. Nobody was gaining land or fighting for a cause. It was just children throwing stones at each other and seeing who could get least hurt."

George avoids looking at me and moves a knight on the board to a position which doesn't benefit him in the game, he isn't paying attention to it.

"It fucked up all of our lives!" I shout, maybe a little too loudly, probably turning a few heads in the main room as my voice travels through the doorway. "Jane means nothing to me now." I move a chess piece, pointlessly. "Remember Ali?"

"Of course I remember Ali, everyone remembers Ali. The only one to have ever escaped, he's a legend here…"

"Yeah well…" I say, leaning forward, speaking discreetly, "we will be the next Ali. We're going through with the original plan, you and me."

I have convinced him, he beams a radiant smile.

"Hey," he says, turning over his shoulder to make sure no one's coming in, before turning back to me and pulling out a chocolate bar in purple packaging from his pocket and handing it across the table.

"What's this?" I gasp, my eyes lighting up, snatching it from him and sliding it into my pocket under the table as quickly as possible.

"I have a deal with a guard, Lucas, he's the one that gets our names on the list quite often. I used to know him years and years ago, we went to school together until my parents had to pull me out, like most of the other kids at the age of ten, because it was no longer affordable. He can get me things sometimes," George whispers, smiling with an arrogance. He has never told me about this before so it's as if he has either suddenly really trusted me, which is dangerous to do in The Vault, or he is trying to bribe me and convince me to stick to our plan because he doesn't believe me, or he is being friendly to trick me because he is thinking of running out on me and leaving me here.

I haven't seen a chocolate bar in years. It must be out of date because they are no longer being made, just like most things of the past.

"And here, take this too," he says, leaning over the table and revealing a hip flask, pouring a dark orangey liquid into my open tea flask on the table.

"What is it?" I ask.

"Whiskey. And it's old as hell so it has a proper kick to it," he whispers, chuckling.

I sip from my flask, the mixture of cold tea and strong whiskey is a pleasure. It soothes my throat and at the same time burns my stomach, warming my whole body and creating tingling sensations from my head to my toes.

We tap our flasks together, take another sip each and burst into coughing laughter.

It is the happiest and most attached moment we have had in two years, and we both know neither of us are any clearer as to knowing what the other is thinking.

Chapter 8

Yes, I am making a weapon, I think to myself, glancing over at Harry who sits upright in his bed, perspiring ever since Mohammed had entered and spoken to him. Yes, I am going to use the weapon, I smile to myself, knowing that when Mohammed had looked over at me he had wondered what I was doing under my duvet; that brown bastard knows everything. My grandad had told me as a child that once there was a time when people like Mohammed wouldn't have been seen anywhere in this country, but I was born in a generation that formed multicultural, one-language nations in the west, and since my teenage years you would rarely meet a racist anymore, although even now, even though the world has been split in two, even though there are barely any humans alive, I still hold my views.

Nick is hopeless, that's what they think of me. No one here believes I have the ability to escape, which has to be the most stupid thought of all.

Yes, I know you're planning an escape, I tell Harry in my thoughts. He's sat there, staring into empty space, processing all the information he possesses, and is probably figuring out how to overcome the recent dilemma he has been faced with.

It doesn't take a fucking genius to work out what is going on. Harry has an escape plan and it has something to do with Marcus; the two of them never speak to anyone, yet they seem to have gained a level of communication between them. I had seen Harry handing over the book to Marcus, offering him to read it. He has never before offered anyone to read a book he has been reading and it just so happens to be the same book he had dropped when he had decided to step in for that pussy John and attack me, allowing the pages to be exposed, and I am confident I had seen some form of ink drawing inside, possibly a secret message or a map of some kind. That means that someone has a pen and I believe that to be the silent freak with the cut palms called Marcus who lays in a ball on his bed at this moment.

What Mohammed has to do with all of this I'm not sure, but he made the effort to approach Harry and tell him something, something which has obviously scared Harry as if he has been caught, and he had glanced over to Marcus as if referring to him in conversation. Mohammed had made sure I wasn't listening, and I couldn't hear, but I could tell from my peripheral vision that he had also glanced over to me, and as soon as Bill had entered Mohammed had decided to leave the room as if what they had been talking about was private between them. So as far as I can work it out: Mohammed is either involved in the plan or he has gained knowledge of it and has made Harry aware, just to frighten him.

But unfortunately for them there is now a fourth member involved. That would be me. I know of this information, I have been studying it carefully, therefore, I am going to make them aware I know. No one believes I'm getting out of here? I almost laugh to myself at the thought. I have only been waiting for others around me to form the plans and for me to open my ears to jump in at the best opportunity.

I stop carving the knife underneath my duvet, which is now so finely shaped that I'm confident it could cut through glass, and I sneakily tuck it into my pocket, making sure the edge isn't too close to my dick. I'm going to have to be very careful when I walk and sit, every movement puts me at risk of it tearing through the material and slicing open my flesh.

I climb out of bed and head over to Harry who squints at me as if he's trying to measure me.

"Have you come to apologise for earlier?" he asks. I laugh at that, creating an echo through the room. You shouldn't laugh here because everyone will know you have a reason to be happy, and the only reason that could be is either receiving a letter from a loved one or having an escape plan, and seeing as I have never received a letter my laughter would tell everyone the exact reason why I had laughed. Bill and Marcus both look over their shoulders at me before returning to face their wall.

"No," I reply in a quiet voice, but a quiet voice with power boiling inside of it.

"Then what do you want?"

I'm making him feel anxious, I can tell, and that satisfies me. I have to force myself not to release another burst of laughter.

"I know," I say, whispering. "I know all about it." I wink at him. His face shows fury and fear.

"Fuck off!" he growls.

"If you don't involve me, then I will let *everyone* know about it."

"What?" he questions, sitting himself up. I'm wondering if he is going to jump out of bed and grab me so I rest my hand against the pocket with the knife, making sure it is there, almost to comfort and reassure myself.

"In other words…" I begin, licking my lips with a sly grin, "if you don't involve me then I will make sure everyone wakes up during your exit."

If everyone knows about it, then the spy will know about it and if the spy knows about it then the guards will know about it and if the guards know about it then…yeah, you understand. Harry knows this, he can tell what I mean by the threat.

I don't need to say anything else so I turn away, leaving him there to sweat even more, and I have myself a pleasant little walk into the main room, trying to hide the obvious beaming smile on my face, knowing that I could be leaving tonight.

Chapter 9

Everyone has finished their second meal of the day as the green light glows above The Door, which is open with Lucas and Anthony standing guard by it.

Anthony has just collected all the paper plates and plastic spoons which have been used to serve us all half a tin of cold baked beans each, and he has wheeled the trolley out into the hallway. Two other guards have entered today and they are in the bedroom removing the items such as soap and flasks which belonged to Steve, Samuel and Mark. They are also going to spend the next ten minutes removing the empty beds from The Vault with the help from some of us.

Thankfully for me, George is in there helping the guards lift a bed so I have time to do what I need to do.

"Lucas," I say gently, speaking closely to him not only so no one else can hear but also to make sure he can smell the whiskey on my breath which I had drank earlier with George during the game of chess.

I want Lucas to smell it so he is aware that George shares his luxuries with me and therefore has told me about Lucas's little deceit against his fellow guards.

"Yes?" he asks, looking to me. Anthony glances over and then returns his attention to John, Marcus and Bill who sit in the main room. The others are either in the playroom or assisting the guards in the bedroom.

"You need to make sure that my name on the garden duty list is the one that is chosen for tomorrow's duty."

"Well that's completely based on random selection. It varies each time…"

"No, this time you need to make sure it is me," I order. I can't believe I am giving an order to a guard, he looks bewildered.

Anthony steps away to peer into the bedroom which gives me a perfect chance to speak more clearly and quickly.

"What?" asks Lucas, almost annoyed.

"Make sure I am selected and George isn't. If you do that, then I can supply you with very important information I have gained," I invent.

"You do realise you're bribing a guard?"

"You do realise that the world is over and I couldn't give a fuck?" I respond, agitated. He falls silent and accepts what I am saying.

"I can give you information which you need to know and in return I get a day outside, that's all."

"What's this got to do with George?" he questions.

I look over my shoulder, scan the room, making sure they haven't started carrying a bed out yet, judging how much time I have.

"He can't be on the list, he can't be there tomorrow when I give you the information. It is to do with him. If I'm not chosen for garden duty and he is, then, well…put it this way, I know the two of you are old friends and I know all about you breaking the rules by giving him extra treats…"

"Now you're threatening a guard…"

"No one in this world has authority now, so fuck your laws and dominance," I reply, growling beneath my warmed alcohol breath. "Just do as I say or there is going to be trouble."

Lucas looks stunned and is shrinking inside, his own pupils falling down two black holes. He nods in agreement.

"I need to send mail," I say.

"That's rare for you…"

"It's rare for anyone. Just hurry up!"

Lucas pulls out a sheet of paper, an envelope and a pen from his inside jacket pocket.

I make sure that George hasn't left the bedroom, but I can see through the doorway that a bed has been lifted, the one opposite mine which had belonged to Samuel, and they're trying to rotate and manoeuvre with one another to get it through the doorway to carry out.

I lean against the wall and quickly write in a scribbled, messy fashion on the paper: ***Garden duty tomorrow. Be there. Love Elliott xxx***

Then I fold the paper and slip it inside the envelope before sealing it and writing Jane's full name in the centre in bold letters.

"There," I say, gasping as if I have just run a marathon, something which people used to do in the old days, and I hand him the envelope and pen which he puts inside his pocket.

"Is that all?" Lucas asks, sternly and agitated.

"Just make sure my name is on the list and his isn't, and make sure that letter is sent today."

I turn away, knowing Lucas will be watching me with anger and a sense of not having control, and I hope that everything will work out the way I intend.

Hope is a dangerous concept in a world that possesses so little of it.

I sit down on the centre bench and watch as the beds are carried out one by one.

Chapter 10

The empty beds have all been removed, the guards have departed from The Vault and The Door has been locked.

I am standing by the windows in the main room, smoking my last cigarette of the day with one hand and tapping my coin in my pocket with my other hand, and looking out into the distance, as far as I can look anyway, picturing the image of myself being beyond these walls, beyond the compound of the gardens and beyond the dome.

I study my cigarette and think to myself about how nobody has attempted an escape by using the matches we are provided with. Surely if one of us was to set fire to our clothes or the books in the playroom then the guards would have to enter The Vault and evacuate us, and if all of us were to charge at the same time then surely two or three of us would get away? It's a plan but it's not a plan that guarantees a successful escape. No plan guarantees a successful escape, but the one I already have in mind is the one that has the best chance of getting me out of here, it already worked for someone else so it should work for me.

The escape plan I intend to use, my ticket out of here, the one which Samuel had used, the one which is hovering over those in the playroom who are unaware of it, the one which the guards know nothing about, is waiting for me.

"We have a dilemma," comes a voice from behind. I spin round to see Harry standing there; bulky, red and sweaty. He's in a panic.

"You look like you've just seen a ghost," I reply. Not the wisest term to use in this day and age after all the deaths on Earth, people deem it to be offensive.

"We have a serious fucking dilemma," Harry repeats, this time more desperate. His fists are clenching and he's eyeballing the room.

"What?" I ask, genuinely worried. What problem can he have that is a problem of mine?

"Nick knows," he whispers.

"What?" I gasp, looking around only to realise that Nick isn't present.

"Nick knows about it all. My problem is now your problem. You solve it or you won't be invited, I'll make sure of that."

"Okay okay," I reply, putting a hand out as if to come across as sincere.

Harry seems to think that Nick being aware of his and Marcus's escape plan tonight affects me because he thinks that I want to be a part, and by using Nick's threat on me to do something about it he believes is almost his way of regaining control over me and accepting my place in the queue.

"I'm not joining you anyway," I say. Harry looks confused. "I only told you I knew to make you aware of it, that's all."

"For what reason?"

"Just in case I needed a way out, but it just so happens that I'm no longer interested. I have my own ticket out."

"You're lying…"

"I'm not," I say, biting my teeth to show my annoyance and seriousness.

Harry now looks even more worried, knowing there was no need for him to tell me and that it doesn't affect me.

"I'm afraid it's your problem," I say, returning to look out of the window and smoke my cigarette.

"Not exactly."

"What?" I turn my head, resting my chin on my arm that rests against the window sill.

"If you're telling me that you plan to escape from here," he whispers, once again examining the room, "the last thing you need is for Nick to fuck up mine and Marcus's plan and for the guards to catch us. They'll raid the entire Vault and might possibly find your route. He's told me he'll mouth it if I don't let him join. You can't take that kind of risk, can you?" he blinks repeatedly, praying to himself that he has put a thought into my head. It has worked, now I am worried.

"Okay, I'll do something about it," I reply.

"You promise?"

"Yes, I promise." A mutual trusting between two people. That's something which doesn't ever happen here.

Harry nods at me. The sweat is leaking from his skin, I'm no longer sure if it's just anxiety or if he has some kind of fever.

I take one last puff of the cigarette, drop it onto the ground and stamp it out, glance out the window knowing that what I am about to do may impede me from ever leaving, but I have no choice.

I am heading into the bedroom, with every step I take my heart thumps against my chest, pounding against it like a hammer on a brick wall, or like myself pounding against The Door, desperate to be free. I am doing the only thing there is to do.

The equation is being calculated in my head. The escape plan minus the guards knowing minus the spy informing minus the subject (Nick) revealing = the escape plan being successful.

I am not going to confront Nick, he will be dealt with by removing the middle man from the equation. The spy.

I pass Yung-Lee and Ben on their beds, then I pass Nick and John. I pass Harry. I come to the end of the bedroom, to my left is Marcus and to my right is Bill.

I head right.

All eyes are on me.

Bill is curled over facing the wall.

I don't hesitate, lean over and dig my hand into the inside pocket of his jacket. He wakes up, turns his head on his wrinkly neck and peers up at me in fright.

I don't say a word and pull out the pet rat he keeps, then head back the other way and to the toilet room. I drop the rat into the toilet of the first cubicle and flush it, having to almost push it down, blocking the toilet with water rising to the top of the bowl.

I return to the bedroom, wiping my wet hands in my trousers, and stand in the doorway.

"What was that all about?" someone calls, I can't tell who.

"That was your spy," I answer.

I am met with silence.

All eyes are on Bill. They have some questions to ask.

That's what I have known about Bill. He is the spy. The exact reason he has always attempted to convince everyone that there is no point in escaping because there is nothing out there for us. The rat had just been a microphone which was used to transmit conversations back to the guards. Without that there is no communication between them and Bill, therefore there is no risk of them discovering Harry and Marcus's escape tonight if Nick is to open his mouth, and therefore there is no risk of the guards becoming suspicious, raiding The Vault and discovering Samuel's escape route.

I turn my back on the room, head to the playroom where I ask Kris for a cigarette, careful not to be tempted to glance at the escape route I know of, and then head back to the windows in the main room to smoke and dream.

Chapter 11

It's getting late in the evening, everyone has gone to bed apart from me.

I've just had myself a shower. I prefer having one at night because it's quiet and I can have some peaceful, refreshing time to myself.

Everyone here thinks of me as the man who can't defend himself. John the weakling.

"Bless you God for this water you provide," I whisper, knowing that He gives me strength, as I dry my body with a towel.

Suddenly, a hand wraps round my mouth from behind and another hand reaches round and holds a sharp object to my throat.

"Don't you make a fucking sound!" a voice whispers in my ear, fiercely, placing the edge of the handmade knife against my Adam's apple.

Tears are falling from my face. I am certain that Nick is going to hurt me. Why else would he have come out here at night to find me?

"Whatever it is you want…" I murmur beneath his hand in a muffled voice which is almost inaudible, attempting to bargain with him.

"I want you," Nick replies. He may be behind me but I know he is smirking with an ugly expression of violence, desire and satisfaction. "I'll be leaving soon," he says, lowering me to the ground, forcing me to lay flat on the wet tiled surface with the shower head above dripping on me, one hand on my head, the other with the tip of the knife digging into my abdomen.

"I just wanted to do one thing before I left, something for you to remember me by," he says, now unzipping his trousers.

I am praying to God to take me away from here, to strike me down now, to stop the pain, to forgive me for being so selfish and weak.

Nick holds my head down as he penetrates me, frantically and vigorously thrusting himself in and out of me, causing my anus to tighten from the agony. I'm sure it is bleeding. My scream is trapped in the back of my throat, my tears are glassing over my eyes, and his knife is digging into my stomach.

If I try and fight, he will kill me. I don't mind dying anyway.

"You fucking…dirty…bitch…" he gasps with pacing breath as he continues to rape me.

I hear him pleasurably groan as he clenches my hair and pushes as hard as he can into me, then slaps my face and curses me out of shame, before pulling himself away, zipping up his trousers and preparing to leave me here on the floor like some dirty waste that has been abandoned on the side of a road, with blood and semen now dripping from my anus, and my squirming flesh and breaking tears not knowing how to react.

"You fucker!" comes a bellowing scream as I roll over in fright and pull a towel over myself.

It had been Harry, he has entered the shower room.

He punches Nick who falls to the ground and loses his grip on the knife, then he throws him across the room where he slams into a wall and slumps to the ground.

Harry punches him once, twice, again and again, over and over, blood is gushing from his nose and lips, two teeth have been ripped from their gums and chatter along the tiles, and his eyes are beginning to bruise and swell like two ripe plums.

Several others who have been awoken have come rushing in and stand in the doorways, looking onto the scene and wondering what has happened.

Harry strikes him twice in the ribs with powerful blows from his boot before he turns away. He begins to approach me when all of a sudden Nick crawls along the ground, grabs the knife and before anyone can shout or react, Harry spins round in response to everyone's expression, Nick stabs him in the stomach.

"We should call the guards!" someone cries, I think it might have been George.

"No!" demands Harry, turning round to everyone, holding his stomach where blood oozes through his t-shirt and runs between the gaps in his fingers.

Nick had stabbed him only once before dropping the knife and falling back from the lack of strength; his beating has knocked him half-unconscious.

Harry leans over him and grabs him by the throat. Most others return to the bedroom, not wanting to get involved, but probably wondering if Harry is going to kill Nick.

Chapter 12

"Are you not going to tell the guards? You need medical attention," says Mohammed, who is behind me, along with Marcus.

"No," I reply, my hand squeezing round Nick's neck. The temptation to snap it is overwhelming, but I know I can't because if the escape tonight doesn't go to plan and for some reason I have to stay in The Vault and then tomorrow morning the guards discover Nick's body then it is possible that someone will tell them I was responsible, and then who knows that would happen to me?

I had wanted to leave what felt like an hour ago, everyone seemed to be asleep, apart from Marcus who would have been ready for the escape of course, but then I realised John wasn't in bed and then I saw Nick climb out of bed minutes later. It had been too much of a risk to make my move, so instead I had decided to find out what Nick was doing, being wary of him after he had told me that he was aware of the plan, and I had found him in here attacking John.

"I can't go into care because I am leaving tonight," I say, well aware that John is present, the only person here who doesn't know about my escape, but sure enough that he is in a different state of mind to give a shit about any escape plan someone might have. "The escape is tonight, it can't be changed, isn't that right Marcus?"

"That's right," he replies timidly but strangely confidently. It's the first time the other three in the room: Mohammed, Nick and John, have ever heard his voice.

"And if I leave Marcus on his own then this piece of fucking shit will intervene," I spit the words out, my hand tightening around Nick's throat as his eyes bulge.

"No he won't," says Mohammed. "Because if he does…" he continues, bending down by my side and facing Nick who has our shadows looming over him, "then the rest of us will tell the guards that he raped John and stabbed you, which will put his fate in the unknown."

"Why are you protecting them…?" gasps Nick within my left my hand.

"Because I don't like you," replies Mohammed, leaning into him, "none of us do. You've put yourself in a dangerous position, knowing that any single one of us here might just decide to smother you in the night." Mohammed pauses briefly. "You might as well admit to us, after your attempt to kill Harry, that you were the person who smothered that man about four months ago after your argument over the playroom chairs, weren't you?"

Nick doesn't flinch for a moment but then, whilst we are all looking to him, he nods without expression.

I release him, leaving him on the ground. He is too badly hurt to even attempt to escape tonight anyway, he can barely raise his head or move his arms.

"Speak to John," I whisper to Mohammed. "Make sure he's alright."

Mohammed nods at me.

"Go back to bed, the plan remains the same," I tell Marcus who nods in understanding.

I turn round to Nick who glances up at me with a struggle. Blood that flows from both of us has stained the water on the tiles and is running down the drains.

"By the time I leave the toilet you'd better be lying in bed, otherwise I'll finish you off," I warn, pointing to him. "Do you think you can manage to get there by yourself?"

Nick nods and begins to crawl across the floor.

I pick up the knife and pocket it before going to the toilet room where I remove my t-shirt and examine my open wound in the mirror. It's a two-inch slash, the flesh is stringy from the jagged weapon that had entered and blood is continuously running down my stomach.

I turn on a tap and splash water onto the wound, then I collect some toilet paper from the first cubicle where I briefly notice the toilet is blocked from when Mohammed had flushed the rat.

Bill had to explain to us all earlier about the rat and Mohammed had explained to me in private to let me know that mine and Marcus's escape plan was safe.

I use the toilet paper to dab the wound and try to clean up the blood although it still flows from my insides, and then I stick about ten sheets against my wet skin to cover the wound and the blood instantly begins to seep through them. Then I tear my t-shirt in half and wrap it round my body and use the sleeves to form a tight knot round my back.

I return to the shower room to realise that Nick is no longer here, nor is Mohammed or Marcus, but John is. He hasn't moved, still cowering against the tiled wall under the showerheads with a towel over his abused body.

"John?" I whisper.

"I just want to be alone for a while," he replies. I nod to him in sorrow and head to the doorway when he says quietly, "so long…"

I continue to the bedroom with a momentary smile that quickly vanishes.

Time passes. I'm not sure how long, but it feels like maybe an hour has passed since I got into bed. John hasn't returned and I'm sure Nick is awake and is trying to listen to me in the darkness, and Mohammed is trying to listen to Nick, but I decide it's time.

I have my jacket on, zipped up to my neck, with the t-shirt still wrapped round my body underneath.

I have lost a portion of blood which has stained the sheets of my bed and I feel sick.

In the message, Marcus had told me to wait for the final person to get into bed and to then count to a thousand before crawling to his where I would find him and the escape.

Well, it is now or never, John could be out there all night.

I gently remove the duvet from over me and spin my legs out of bed, placing my feet on the ground to face Bill who has his back to me and is snoring. He may have been the spy but he is no longer a threat without the rat. I try as hard as I can not to make any noise from the bed creaking, it doesn't help that I'm a heavy guy.

I lower myself out of bed and to the ground, then I crawl like a tortoise through the path between mine and Bill's bed, cross the open space in the middle of the room, and head over to the path opposite between Hal's and Marcus's beds.

I turn to the right where Marcus's bed is and lie flat, sliding myself along the ground using my elbows, cursing in my head and holding my tongue flat from the agony that is caused by scraping my stomach against the surface.

As long as I don't pass out now and wake up tomorrow morning with everyone surrounding me, I think to myself.

Suddenly, a hand lands on my shoulder and it causes me to jerk but I'm instantly reassured to see that it's Marcus in his bed. My heartbeat slows down gradually and I am able to retain myself.

He doesn't speak, but instead he slithers out of his bed with his weightless body and joins me on the floor in the pitch black.

As long as no one wakes up now, especially Hal who sleeps beside Marcus.

Marcus must have been awake the whole time just waiting and listening out for me.

As if out of nowhere a small glow appears on the wall underneath his bed which has the letter **X** marked in black ink.

The glow is coming from a small pocket torch which Marcus is now holding, it's not bright or powerful enough to cause any reflection in the room or, from where we are, to form any shadow which others might be able to see.

"Push it," he whispers gently in my ear, so faintly it takes me a few seconds to realise what he has said.

I use both hands outstretched in front of me to push lightly against the wall where the marking is, whilst lying on my stomach like a helpless, squirming insect.

A section of the wall, less than one foot high and two foot wide, comes loose and falls through to the other side without creating much noise, only a light slap which causes the two of us to freeze, waiting to hear for anyone who may have been woken.

Marcus crawls ahead of me through the wall and soon after, with some agonising pain and the certainty that I am leaving a trail of blood behind, I follow him onto the other side.

Chapter 13

Whilst Marcus and Harry were escaping in the bedroom, John was sitting on the floor of the shower room.

He still hadn't moved since the incident, he hadn't even changed into any clothes.

He just sat there, staring at the tiled wall opposite him, with one showerhead above him dripping onto his head every few seconds.

There was shame in his mind, misery in his heart and pain in his body.

John didn't speak to himself, he didn't even speak to God.

In his pile of clothes, he found his trousers, whilst remaining in a sitting position, and he took out a tin of baked beans from one of the pockets.

He had stolen the tin from the trolley earlier when they had had their second meal. The tin was empty. After it had been eaten out of, he had decided to hide it in his pocket which he later on had washed out and kept for himself. He wasn't sure why. What use did it have? It had just been an act of impulse, wanting to have something, a possession of his own.

Now he believed his impulse had been by the hand of God, He had guided him. John now understood why he had taken it. It had a use.

Without thought or fear, believing that God was by his side, John sliced the lid of the tin in two clean swipes, one down the length of each arm from wrist to elbow, and then he lay back as his blood gushed from him. He could feel his soul leaving his body and floating out of The Vault, out of the dome and beyond.

This was his escape. This was his freedom.

A single tear ran down his cheek and there was a faint smile on his face as he closed his eyes.

Part III: The Exit

Day 743

Chapter 1

Harry and I have made it to the edge of the compound. After climbing through the wall we found ourselves inside a small room of pipes; the heat was overwhelming, the steam was intoxicating and there was a gentle humming which wasn't loud enough to be heard from inside The Vault.

We headed through a fire exit out onto an outside balcony with swirling steps that led from the height of the building to the bottom.

When we reached the bottom, Harry being much slower than me with one hand constantly planted on his stomach, we were on ground level in the gardens.

There would be guards patrolling the area, we knew that, so we had to move like stealth soldiers through the bushes until we finally reached the edge of the dome on a mound of grass covered by trees.

Whoever is in charge here is attempting to grow the trees in order to rebuild a community, or so it appears. But we don't care about community, we care about our freedom.

I had been cutting the wall out for several weeks by using an old razor I had managed to hide after they had banned all sharp objects, and seeing as the wall only happened to be plasterboard I realised it could be cut fairly easily.

It had occurred to me that the wall on the far side of the room was plasterboard which was painted to look like a brick wall. I realised this one day when I had climbed into bed a little too heavily, knocking my knee into the wall and noticing it was hollow. My knee had left a dent in the wall which just peeped above my mattress height, which I had been hiding, since, by pushing my duvet as close up to it as I could, not wanting anyone else to figure out what I had discovered.

The best time to cut was when some people were on garden duty, to lower the numbers slightly, and when the rest were in the showers or playroom, and I would sneak under my bed for only twenty or thirty seconds at a time to cut a little deeper, quite often slipping and cutting myself: the reason I have so many scars on my palms.

Harry had asked me where I had got the torch from and I told him I had stolen it from a guard's pocket one day when they had entered with our midday meal and when they hadn't been looking. Pre-The Bomb I had been very poor and had resorted to pickpocketing, something which I had become extremely good at. I'm so quiet I can move like a mouse. Harry also asked me why I had chosen to message him and asked him to join me, and I told him that I needed someone who minded their own business so I was sure they could keep quiet, and he was the only one. To be honest, once I had started cutting through the wall several weeks ago and had begun putting a plan together, the thought of leaving on my own terrified me, so about a month ago, I decided I was going to start messaging one of the others in The Vault to join me, but I was only going to reveal myself once I was confident the person could be trusted (yes, I put trust in him) and once the plan was almost complete.

It is very cold outside (although being inside the dome isn't technically outside) even with the lighting that dimly glimmers in the glass, providing the only source of heat, as the temperature has dropped in recent years since the war; the debris clouding over the sky and blocking out the sun. Luckily we both have our jackets on, although we both know it probably won't make a difference on the outside.

"We left a lot later than we had planned, the sun will be coming up soon," I say, gasping for breath, speaking carefully, looking around in the darkness at all times, the dome's lighting not bright enough to cast a shadow.

"What we have left of the sun," Harry replies, lying beside me on the grass.

"Then let's move," I retort, going head first into the hole that I have been digging for the last three nights when others have been asleep. It's almost a pathway that leads underneath the dome and to the outside, you have to crawl under to fit through though. It had taken me the whole first night just to dig downwards to find the end of the glass which is about two foot under the soil.

For the last three nights I had climbed out of bed when I was sure the last person had fallen asleep, crawled through the hole in the wall, gone through the pipe room and out the fire exit, down the stairs, through the gardens to this area which I had marked with my pen on a tree, using the torch to guide myself. On the first night I had searched for the softest soil in the area, which I believe to be here, where roots had grown underneath the dome from an old bush which I had easily pulled out, dragging out great clumps of soil with them, and by using my hands for the last three nights I had managed to dig out a hole large enough to fit a person through. Three nights! And I know Elliott and George have been digging theirs for months: with the help of two of them and with the use of garden tools.

I know about their plan, it's pretty obvious: they are always going on garden duty and they are always talking an awful lot, and they always come back with more dirt under their fingernails than anyone else.

Each night I returned once it started getting slightly lighter, it was difficult to tell because it was always a shade of dark, and I would shower before everyone else so no one would notice the soil on my hands and then sit in a cubicle with my sponge to scrub any soil off my clothes, which I'd pour town a toilet. By the first meal of the day I was exhausted which was the reason why I spent a lot of my days in bed.

"No," cries Harry. "You go!"

"What?" I ask, pulling my head back out of the hole after breathing in the air from the outside world, the old world. I have to say, it doesn't smell good or clean. I had even seen my breath in front of me being carried away like an iceberg floating in the darkness and the tip of the dome had brushed my neck like an icicle, causing me to shiver as pimples appeared on my skin and the hairs on my body erected.

"I can't go any further," he states, lying his head back on the grass as I shine the torch on him and notice he has opened his jacket and untied the t-shirt underneath that had been wrapped round his stab wound. There are soaking wet, bloody paper towels stuck to his skin, and the blood has leaked straight through and stained his stomach. It is everywhere.

"But…I can help, you'll…"

"No," he says, shaking his head, giving in, accepting, and being final. "No," he repeats.

I want to cry, it is the first time I have felt emotion for another person since losing my family and friends to the war. I hold Harry's hand.

"Thanks for giving me a chance," he says, his voice is becoming weaker and his eyes are struggling to stay open.

"I'm sorry," I reply.

"Go! Now! Whilst you have time! Go!" he calls.

I crawl through the hole underneath the dome and don't look back, leaving Harry behind as he bleeds to death, and I flee out into the icy conditions, into the distance where everything seems blacker and darker than any night in history, into the unknown.

Chapter 2

The guards have just been to confirm that they found Harry's body this morning, he had a stab wound and was lying dead next to an escape hole, and he had had the sharp object in his pocket, but they didn't believe it was suicide and they ruled out the other escapee from being the guilty murderer. Marcus, they tell us, has gone.

I could have been gone too, I think to myself, as I sit on the centre bench in the main room with my beaten and bruised face from what Harry had done to me, looking around to see the numbers in The Vault getting smaller.

The guards take away John's body after we discovered it this morning and they class it as suicide but they feel suspicious.

They tell us that John was raped and ask us who did it. Nobody speaks. My heart is pouncing into my throat, I'm afraid I'm going to choke on it and suffocate on my own vomit.

They then discover more blood in the shower room which isn't near John's body, also in the toilet room and on the bedroom floor which leads a trail to the escape route underneath Marcus's bed, indicating that the blood belongs to Harry and therefore he must have been stabbed before the escape, inside The Vault. They ask who did it. Nobody speaks. My heart is having a race, I'm afraid it's going to suddenly lose control and attack my system.

The guards block up the escape route in the wall by screwing on a steel sheet on the other side before they remove Marcus's, Harry's and John's beds. There are only ten remaining.

They ask if anyone feels unsafe and if so then they can leave now and be taken to another floor to live. Hal, Roger and Yung-Lee all stand and leave. Seven remaining.

This tells the guards that the rapist and murderer is still in The Vault seeing as the three that left were all happy to leave together.

They ask one more time if anyone would like to admit to it and if anyone knows anything. Nobody speaks. My heart is now going to explode, I'm certain.

I can't die here, I tell myself.

"We'll find you," Anthony says, smiling as he peruses his eyes around the room, landing his focus on me.

Everyone inside here hates me and the guards are waiting to fuck me, I think to myself.

I have to leave. Today.

Chapter 3

"Ah…my last one," I say aloud with my cigarette packet exposed, purposely wanting George to see and hear me.

"Here," he replies, handing me three cigarettes which I put inside my packet. "For the road," he says, smiling and winking.

"Thanks," I say, feeling a little guilty. I would need a couple on my journey away from here and I knew he had plenty. I know that I will be leaving George behind, this will be our last time together, as long as Lucas has done as I said. I ate half the bar of chocolate, that George gave me, in bed this morning before everyone woke up, making sure I would be ready and energised for today, followed by carrying out some of my exercising, then having a shower so I'll smell and look as good as I can for Jane, and now I am crossing my fingers in hope.

"Now for garden duty," calls Lucas. "Unfortunately Number 637 is no longer with us," he says, referring to John. "Numbers 641…" Ben steps forward with a grin, I am praying for my name, George is probably praying it isn't mine, "…and 649." I step forward, hiding my grin.

"What are you going to do?" whispers George in my ear.

"I'll just do ordinary gardening today to divert any attention from the hole," I reply, lying through my teeth and speaking so quickly it must be obvious that I don't care and I'm desperate to get out of here.

"Ben had garden duty two days ago," argues George to Lucas.

"So did you," Lucas responds, smiling, putting the list away in his pocket.

"Well can't I step in for John's space?"

"No, once the list is confirmed that is it, there are no late volunteers, I'm sorry."

George tries to speak in private to Lucas, "But…"

137

"I couldn't this time," whispers Lucas, "it's the way it works. Next time."

I'm standing behind George, staring at Lucas with wide eyes and an open mouth, shaking my head, signalling him not to give anything away and to remember our deal.

"But…" George begins to argue.

"He said your name isn't on the fucking list so fuck off," barks Anthony, shoving George back.

"I'll see you later," I say, joining Ben in a queue behind the guards.

"Sure," George replies, watching me leave through The Door as it closes and locks.

"So what's this information you have then?" asks Lucas as we head down the hall of the building with Anthony leading Ben in front.

"George is going to escape today, I'm not sure how, but he is," I reveal, lying, attempting to distract any attention from me, having to hand over the only person who is the closest resemblance to a friend that I have had in the last two years for my own survival.

When we are outside, the guards hand Ben and me a shovel, a fork, a pair of plyers, and a bag of seeds each, and tell us to head into the gardens and care for the land. We have three to four hours and then we'll be called back by the whistle, if we are not back in time then we could face punishment. This is always the same drill on garden duty, their threat is false. George and I had been late on many occasions when we had gotten carried away with digging our hole and had never received any punishment, all you have to say is that you were enjoying the luxury of nature so much and the guards laugh and tell you you're being spoilt.

"I know you have a plan," Ben whispers to me as we head off into the greenery. "Today seems to be the day that everyone has their plan in place. Good luck!"

He then runs off into the bushes, and although he is a little fat, which means he had been richer than most of us in the past life seeing as he could afford to eat plenty; he runs fairly quickly, dropping his plyers, seeds and fork on the way but carrying the shovel, disappearing with a plan in his mind.

I make sure I am deep inside the greenery, surrounded by trees and bushes, nettles and thorns, and that the buildings are all out of view, meaning hopefully I am out of view from the guards, before I throw my gardening equipment into a bush and hide behind a tree to wait.

Several minutes pass and I start panicking, when all of a sudden there she is, she has arrived as we had agreed. We knew where to meet because this is the path everyone takes to do garden duty, so all I had to do was wait for her to walk by.

Jane, with her beautiful long brown hair, her dark eyes and her luscious lips. Her figure had always been slim but is much slimmer now, almost in an unhealthy condition, but she still remains as attractive to me as ever.

I grab her and pull her behind the tree where she is stunned to see me; our hands on each other's skin for the first time in two years, our eyes gazing into each other's, our lips touching gently and our hands caressing one another's bodies.

The women's clothing is similar to ours as they wear black jackets, white t-shirts and black shoes, but instead of just blue jeans they have the choice of them or blue skirts. Jane wears a blue skirt, which I now raise as I remove her pants whilst sliding my other hand under her top and squeezing her breasts as she pulls down my jeans, and we continue kissing as we make love against that tree.

"I love you Jane," I whisper in her ear.

"I love you Elliott," she replies, gasping and groaning.

I give her the other half of the chocolate bar George had given me, the half I hadn't eaten in bed this morning and had saved for her. She looks amazed to see it in her hands, her smile forever extends and she hugs me jubilantly before she eats it as fast as she can and throws the wrapper to the side. Surely there's no such thing as littering now? I think to myself and giggle.

We then wash our faces and drink from a small stream of water that runs beside us, it is refreshingly clean and pure. Then we discover a couple of red apples growing in a tree, pluck them and eat them, they are sweet and crunchy. Whoever is in charge here, I ponder, is trying to grow new plants and fruits to restart a community that none of us want to be a part of, because we are confined, we want our freedom. Jane and I smoke a cigarette each, which I had taken from George, whilst we sit behind a bush and speak quietly, holding each other and constantly exchanging eye contact and passionate kisses.

The grass is greener on the other side, I think to myself.

"Shit, we'd better go," I pant, realising we have probably been an hour already.

Seconds after I speak, there comes the sound of crunching twigs and leaves under walking feet.

If we are caught without gardening equipment, then they will know something suspicious is happening, and I then wonder whether the law that had been implemented in 2055 banning all sexual intercourse still exists, even after the world has more or less ended, and I realise it is a possibility based on the fact that men and women are separated in this new community that is slowly being constructed inside the dome.

I reflect on the fact that it will take years before anyone is allowed to walk freely in these gardens and do as they please. *If* that ever happens.

Peeking over the bush, I see a guard walking by, having himself a stroll through the garden, wearing the usual military uniform and carrying a machine gun...

Four Hours Later

Chapter 4

"And Number 649 has escaped and won't be returning," says Anthony.

I knew it, I knew he had gone. I knew the bastard was going to run out on me and leave me behind. I knew he had lied, I knew he had been planning something against our plan and I knew he had betrayed me to be with that woman. I had known something bad had happened because the gardeners should have returned two or three hours ago.

I am standing at the windows of the main room, gazing out, wondering where Elliott will be right now, wondering if the hole has been found yet and filled in, wondering when or if I will leave this place, full of rage and bitterness. I had stupidly put trust in someone here, which had been the ultimate mistake.

The guards have just entered for the second meal of the day and to inform us of Ben and Elliott's successful departures.

There are only five remaining: Bill, Nick, Mohammed, Kris and myself (George).

Anthony is just wheeling the trolley out into the hallway when all of a sudden Nick jumps to his feet, launches the contents of his flask (recently boiled tea) into Lucas's face, who cries out in agony, losing his sight and concentration, and Nick grabs the pistol from Lucas's belt, and without thought or emotion, he points it at Anthony's head and fires a single bullet.

Anthony flies backwards into The Door which is now open, his brains and blood splattered against it as he sinks to the floor, whilst Lucas wipes at his face and struggles to defend himself as his steaming skin turns red and blotchy, and in the meantime Nick flees out into the hallway and is gone, whilst myself and the other three stand in the main room and see it all happen in a blur without responding.

It's tempting for us to leave, but before long four guards appear in the doorway with their guns pointed. When they find Anthony dead and Lucas in pain they tell the four of us to stand at the windows with our backs to them and our hands on our heads, whilst they clean up the mess and deal with the situation, knowing that someone has taken a guard's gun, killed a guard and fled The Vault.

"Elliott ran on me," I whisper to Mohammed who stands by me. "We had a plan together and he ran out on me."

"I know," Mohammed replies. "Don't worry, I have something you can join."

"How do I trust anyone now?"

Nobody trusts anyone here. That is a lie. Of course I trusted Elliott, there's no other word for it.

"Well, you'll just have to if you ever want to get out of here," says Mohammed. "I'm leaving tonight, so if you want to leave then I'll save you a ticket."

Chapter 5

The guards tell us that there is nothing out there for us, that we are safe here, that we have a chance of surviving here and living a life, and that none of us should attempt any more escapes.

Nobody listens. We don't care what they tell us, we want out.

Mohammed and George are leaving together, they've been talking about it to Bill and myself.

"You can join too, Kris," said Mohammed.

"No, I have my own thing," I told them.

Bill begged to join them and Mohammed arranged for the three of them to leave together.

We're talking open to one another now, being honest, revealing things, because it no longer seems to matter seeing as there are only four of us remaining.

But I have my own thing, that's what I told them, and it's true. Everyone here had always just seen me as Kris, the guy with the card tricks, but in actual fact I used to be a magician and I know more than just a trick or two.

In the two years of being here, I have been tricking people by allowing them to believe I enjoy playing card games. I do enjoy playing card games, I have spent most of my time doing that since being in The Vault, but actually all along I have been building a plan, blinding them with illusions when actually it's my way of escaping.

This afternoon I gather Mohammed, George and Bill round the table in the playroom and I hand out a set of cards.

Minutes later, whilst they're busy focusing on their hand they've been dealt and trying to listen to the rules of the game, I show them a magic trick.

And I disappear. I vanish. I'm gone from there. Out of The Vault, no doors or walls confining me, I'm free from this place, beyond the gardens, on the other side of the dome, on the outside.

The world is a shit place, I soon discover that, and I'm not sure how long I can survive, but we'll see, and I guess you'll never find out what happens to me.

One other thing you'll never find out is how I managed to escape, how I managed to fool the others with a card trick.

A magician never reveals his secrets.

Chapter 6

Ten minutes after fleeing The Vault with a pistol and the blood of Anthony's on his clothes, and after having managed to take the stairs to the bottom floor without another guard passing by the whole time, Nick had made it outside and had been strolling through the gardens, clambering over bushes and stamping on plants.

He hadn't been seen by a guard because there weren't many of them. Even if he had been caught escaping, he wouldn't have been shot. This was due to the fact that inside the complex the 'guards' did not refer to themselves as guards, they were in fact carers. So if he had been caught, the carers would have used their weapon to regain control over him, most of the weapons weren't even loaded, Nick had gotten lucky with the pistol he had, and they would have escorted him to another floor where he would be locked inside again to live. This was the same case with anyone that had an escape plan or to have assisted in one and was reported by a spy, and to anyone who may have caused other trouble inside their living space; they were simply taken away by the carers and sent to live on another floor in one of the buildings.

Nick came to a section that seemed to be blocked off from the rest of the compound, as if no one was supposed to enter.

It was far too tempting and after the excitement of killing another man and running away Nick couldn't resist going into territory he wasn't supposed to.

He tucked the pistol into his trousers and began climbing the wired fence which was about sixteen foot high, surrounded by the tallest trees in the gardens which were cared for by the carers in order for none of the survivors to be aware of this restricted area and to keep them away.

Whatever is this place? Nick thought, as he reached the top, then feeling the pistol come loose from his trousers and watching it fall to the ground with a thud.

"Shit," he whispered to himself, but decided against going back down to retrieve it, he was already at the top and needed to move fast if he wanted to escape.

He began to believe that this would lead to an exit from the dome and started laughing silently to himself as he imagined naked women he would hunt down and find in a world that had no law and in a world where he could have all the freedom he was welcome to. He began to think, as he put his legs over and started climbing down the fence on the other side, about everything he could take for himself without anyone telling him he wasn't allowed to. As he came to the ground and was inside the fenced off area he thought of the life he was going to lead, any life he fancied.

When Nick turned round, he realised that the inside of the area was just like the gardens, it was basically another garden which had been separated from the rest and was surrounded with trees and bushes, although it was only a small section.

He took two steps forward when suddenly that smile on his face was removed and the images in his head were swiped.

Two fully grown adult tigers with beautiful orange and white fur and black stripes appeared from behind the bushes and began to approach Nick with curiosity. Their whiskers shined and their eyes burned with magnificence as their giant paws crawled towards him with majestic movements, their tails were swinging back and forth behind them, and they growled whilst studying Nick.

These two tigers had been collected by the army, one male and one female, possibly the last two tigers alive from zoos around the country, and they were being protected as an endangered species, just like the humans, to breed and survive, to be part of the new world. And they, just like humans, were very hungry.

Nick reached for the pistol but remembered it was on the other side of the fence. The movement of his hand reaching into his trousers surprised the tigers and they instantly leapt towards him and locked their jaws into his flesh, pierced his skin with their claws and began to tear him apart. His scream echoed through the gardens causing several carers and gardeners on duty in the area to look over, but by the time they would reach him it would be too late. His limbs were ripped away from his body and his blood rained down onto the grass as the tigers enjoyed their first major meal in a long time.

Chapter 7

"This is how Samuel escaped," I say, standing on top of the table in the playroom with George and Bill below me, watching.

This is the escape I have been waiting to use, the one I have known about since Samuel had managed to get away, the one which I have kept to myself until now.

Why have I told the others? To be honest I feel sorry for George after Elliott abandoned him and I realise it doesn't matter if the others (Kris and Bill) want to join because there's only us left inside The Vault, so it's hardly like someone else is going to intervene and sabotage my plan, besides, there is no longer a spy after I had dealt with Bill's rat.

Kris has disappeared, none of us know or understand how, but he has. I wish him luck.

I reach up to the ceiling and unscrew the frame of the air vent by using the lucky penny from my pocket. The screws were already loose after Samuel had climbed through and must have screwed the frame back on when he was in the vent by putting his hand through the gaps and twisting the screws back in with his fingers.

That's how I had figured he had escaped. Yesterday morning, after it had been confirmed he had escaped, I had gone into the playroom and had noticed a detail that was out of place. The screws were only screwed in half way. I was stunned that no one else had noticed.

I place the frame down on the table and say to George, "Give me a boost."

George climbs up onto the table and bends down with his hands flat on top of one another so I can place one foot on and use his shoulders to keep my balance as he lifts me up. I grab onto the ledge in the square opening of the ceiling where I pull myself up and inside the vent. It's tight and warm but it's an exit.

"Now you," I say to George, as I place one hand on the vent and hang one hand down.

George leaps up and grabs onto the vent with one hand and my hand in his other as I pull him up, and he gains enough leverage to hoist himself inside the vent.

It then occurs to me that Samuel couldn't have escaped by himself. He wouldn't have been able to reach the vent by jumping from the table and he hadn't used a chair otherwise it would have still been there on the morning after he had disappeared.

It must have been Steve, I think to myself, seeing as he had obviously known about it and the guards had taken him away, obviously having been informed by Bill and his rat. Perhaps Steve was supposed to have escaped with him? Why would he have turned down an open escape opportunity? It doesn't matter now.

"Now me," says Bill, as he struggles to climb onto the table with his weak legs and tired bones.

"Hmm…" I reply, teasing him as George and I stare down at him from the vent. He can't reach us from here even if he leapt, and if he somehow managed to he wouldn't have the strength, even if he used a chair he is too old to be able to pull himself up.

"I didn't want to be a spy, they told me I had to do it or I would be punished, please forgive me," he begs, hoping that he's still welcome in the escape plan and that he can join us.

But that had never been my intention. I had said George and Kris could and had meant it. I don't care about Bill. It's possible that he may bang on The Door and call the guards, informing them that the two of us are escaping, but if he did that it wouldn't benefit him and he knows it. If we're caught and returned to The Vault, then he knows that George and I could kill him for interfering with our chance of freedom, and if we're caught and taken someplace else then he knows he'll be on his own anyway. Besides, the guards will be disappointed with him for being discovered as a spy, they probably wouldn't want to listen to him.

"You've sacrificed too many people and you were willing to sacrifice us," I reply. His face is shrinking along with his body.

"You said that I could join!" he cries.

"Yes, well...I guess that's one thing that hasn't changed about the world: People lie. You can stay here to rot on your own!"

"You fucking bastards!" Bill wails.

George and me turn our backs on him and crawl down the vent as I lead the way, the two of us heading for freedom.

Earlier That Day (Elliott and Jane)

Chapter 8

I do not hesitate. I grapple the guard from behind and use all the strength that remains in my body and transport it through my arm where I lock him round the throat and pull him against me, forcing him to drop the machine gun, and when he does so, I bend over and pick it up, aiming it at him as he coughs to catch his breath. I demand for him to throw me his pistol too which he does. I remove the magazine from the machine gun, noticing that it isn't loaded anyway, but pocket it before throwing the unloaded weapon in a bush several feet away from me. I check the pistol, there are two bullets, and point it in his direction.

"Jane, let's go!" I command.

She comes round from behind the tree and joins me by my side. We walk backwards, me aiming the gun at all times at the guard who now stands still in the middle of the path with both hands raised. It is very possible that an alert has been signalled, he could have some form of communication on him which allows whoever is in charge, or other guards, to hear that he is in trouble and that a couple of people are on the run.

I lead Jane in the direction of the hole that I have been digging for the last four months with George.

At the edge of this part of the dome, there are two bushes which I pull apart; George and I had previously cut the roots which are now dead, meaning the bushes are now only being used to hide the hole.

"I would not have stopped you," says the guard from behind. He has followed us. We turn to him. He isn't with anyone in sight and remains unarmed.

"Then go away," I reply, helping Jane climb through the hole as she gets her hands and clothes covered in dirt.

"I would not advise you to leave!" the guard cries, desperately begging us to stay. "It is my duty to convince you that there is nothing out there that can possibly be worth dying for and that the only chance of a new life is here. We need the numbers to grow in order for the human race to continue. It is your choice, but once you're out there you're on your own, we can't save you and you can't return."

I ignore him although his words terrify me, but I believe he is tricking us, it's his job, he's meant to make sure we stay inside the dome and don't return to the old world where hardly anyone has survived and where nothing exists, but we have to see it for ourselves to believe it.

Jane is on the other side. I climb through with the pistol still in my hand and when I pull myself out and I'm free of the dome, desperate to breathe real air on the real outside, I hear Jane's scream…

There is no outside. There is no air.

"We told you not to go out there!" the guard's cry comes from the hole in the soil as the two of us stand there staring into the distance, as far as we can see through our eyes which feel as if they're being glazed over with ice, which is hard because although it is daytime it feels like night. "Out there is the wasteland!"

From out here it isn't possible to see into the dome because the outside glass seems frozen and is covered in black dust like a cake that has been frosted with death.

"You would have only had to wait a little longer and the two of you would have been reunited!" the guard calls from the other side. "The sexes are separated so once the healthiest have survived then everyone will be partnered to reproduce. They will live together, male and female, amongst each other. Once a new generation has been born and raised, then inside the dome, this new community we have been building for you, will be safe for them to live and start a new world. You would have had the choice of being with whom you wanted! You would have only had to wait a little longer!" he repeats, his voice now breaking with genuine sorrow.

The sound of other footsteps from inside join the guard and then the soil is instantly shovelled back in gradually. They are blocking us out, blocking the old world out.

We freeze, stunned.

The land is dead. Everything is black. There are no trees, the ground has not grown, the sky is murky, and the air is damp and difficult to breathe in.

The guards, The Vault, the gardens, the dome, the new community, whoever is in charge, had not in fact been imprisoning us, it is now clear they had been protecting us. The guns were for control, the separation of sexes was for control, the spy was for control. Anyone that had ever been removed from The Vault wouldn't have been punished or executed, they would have just been moved to another vault. It was clear now. They needed us inside, they needed us to survive, they needed to find as many healthy people as possible to restart the population, but Jane and I have sacrificed our race for our own freedom which does not exist out here.

Jane's hand clutches mine and we restrict from moving a muscle, mesmerised in horror at the scenery we are confronted with; like a portrait of a bleak universe that we belong to.

"We had a beautiful planet," I whisper. "A perfect specimen as our host. We were the disease that killed it."

Anyone that has escaped or does escape, has and will, in fact, committed or be committing suicide, I think to myself.

Jane looks to me, her eyes are suddenly bloodshot and seem to be coated in debris from the reflection of the world that glistens in her teary eyes. Her chest is rising and falling rapidly, as is mine, as we both struggle to access oxygen and feel as if we're being suffocated.

I glance down at the pistol in my other hand and we turn to face each other, nose to nose. I then remember a book my father had told me about when I was a child, he had read it when he was younger when books had been accessible to everyone. It had been called *Romeo and Juliet* and was by someone called William Shakespeare.

There are two bullets in the pistol. One each.

I kiss Jane for the last time.

Epilogue

Somewhere in the south of England, in the countryside, a family of three lived in an underground shelter, just as they had done for the last four years.

There had been a fourth and fifth member of the family. The great-grandfather had died of a heart attack a couple of months ago. The dad had been too unwell at the time to go outside and bury him, so the son volunteered. When he returned, trembling all over and struggling to speak, the others asked him what it was like outside, and he managed to stutter, simply: "Terrible." He died two days later from symptoms relating to pneumonia.

They had been surviving down there on tinned food, most of which was now out of date, and a tap which had a draining system that ran from the house to the shelter, but which they were sure by now was stale, polluted and contaminated. They had been using a bucket as a toilet which the dad emptied each day by opening the door slightly and tipping it out, never allowing much air inside and avoiding studying the world.

The food had all gone some weeks ago just after the son's death. In order for the remaining three to survive, and with the dad deciding that none of them should go outside to bury him due to that being the result of his death, they had no choice but to eat him, although they felt sick eating their own son and brother, and although they felt shame in tearing apart his dignity, his flesh was all they had, and besides, he was decomposing inside the shelter and had begun smelling bad and attracting more bugs than there already were, he had become a health hazard and would cause them all to develop diseases.

The three of them all had dreadful raspy coughs that never soothed and heavy chests which produced harsh breathing. They suffered with aching bones from no longer sleeping or sitting in comfort, and because most of the time they were crouching or in a bent position.

Their skin was dry and they all had blisters, spots and cracks constantly appearing and rarely healing, all because they hadn't had any exposure to the sunlight; this also affected their eyesight which had worsened, especially the dad's, from living in the dark.

They had survived the initial catastrophe after fleeing their home when they had seen the television warning and had driven here to the dad's grandfather's house which supplied the World War Two shelter that had been their home for four years, but if they stayed here any longer they would not survive.

All three of them: Dad, Mum and daughter, wanted to discover what was left of the world. Not much, they imagined. They hadn't seen anything outside of the shelter in all these years.

One morning (they knew it was morning because Dad's watch had continued working all this time) they agreed that they would leave the shelter.

They all wondered if they were the last humans on the planet.

The dad opened the door and the three of them stepped out of the darkness and into the gloom.

The war of 2057, which to many survivors was referred to as the Apocalypse, had caused the skies to blacken, almost creating a constant eclipse.

January–March 2017